CRANNÓG 48 summer 2016

Editorial Board

Sandra Bunting
Ger Burke
Jarlath Fahy
Tony O'Dwyer

ISSN 1649-4865
ISBN 978-1-907017-51-3

Cover image: 'Tempus frangit tempus ducit' by Marie-Jeanne Jacob
Cover image sourced by Sandra Bunting
Cover design by Wordsonthestreet
Published by Wordsonthestreet for Crannóg magazine
www.wordsonthestreet.com @wordsstreet

All writing copyrighted to rightful owners in accordance with The Berne Convention

CONTENTS

The Pier
David Butler 9

A Pentina for my Leopard Coat
Kim Bridgford 15

Night Cycle
Andrew Caldicott 16

Little Pools of Light
Sandra Bunting 18

A Bad Fit
Olivia Fitzsimons 19

Star Anise
Jennifer Waring 22

Thistlecrack
Jane Burn 24

We Are Nothing But Afraid
Natalie Crick 25

The Return Of Her
Clive Donovan 26

Look and See
Sheila Gorman 28

Among The Living
A. Mahlon Reece 32

Who Sent You?
Honor Duff 34

An Ode Spins Through the Night
Saddiq Dzukogi 35

Earworm
Órla Fay 36

Night Cycle
Mary Ellen Fean 37

Teardrops
Martin Keaveney 38

I Was Given
Mary Melvin Geoghegan 44

August In Memoriam
Caitlyn Rooke 45

Principles of Fatherhood
Kevin Graham 46

So I Didn't Stay 'Til The End
S. K. Grout 48
The Beach at Youghal
Edel Hanley 50
Study in Charcoal
Tamzin Mitchell 51
The Sky Confesses
Mark Hart 55
Standing People
Andrea Ward 56
If It Is True That Humans Are Mobile Trees
Deirdre Hines 58
Torn
Pamela Johnson 59
Dusking Through Waves
Wendy Holborow 60
The Best of Both Worlds
Esther Murbach 62
Stickleback
Iain Twiddy 64
Marie-Thérèse Walter Mourns the Death
of her Former Lover Pablo Picasso
Adam Tavel 65
To Choose
Michael G. Smith 66
Seeing The Light
Deirdre Nally 67
Walking Without Snowshoes
John D. Kelly 72
Cochin Hens
Anthony Lawrence 74
A Dog's Life
Mercedes Lawry 76
I, Object
Emily Woodworth 77
A Night at the Theatre
Sean Kelly 83
Not to go Back
Vanessa Kirkpatrick 84

Don Juan in 30 Lines
Craig Kurtz..86
The Dare
Tanya Farrelly..87
Crow
V.P. Loggins...92
The Stone Masons' Yard Revisited
Eamonn Lynskey...93
Snapdragon
Olivia Kenny McCarthy..94
Perfection
Hanahazukashi...95
The Colouring of Eggs
Linda McKenna..98
Magnetism
Mel White..99
Loving The Glass Blower
Cheryl Pearson...100
Single File
Simon Perchik...101
The Crannóg Questionnaire
Mike McCormack..102
Artist's Statement
Marie-Jeanne Jacob...107

Biographical Details 109

The Galway Study Centre

Since 1983, the Galway Study Centre has been dedicating itself to giving an excellent education service to post-primary school students in Galway.

info@galwaystudycentre.ie
Tel: 091-564254

www.galwaystudycentre.ie

BRIDGE MILLS
GALWAY LANGUAGE CENTRE
Established 1987

Small family run language school
ACELS and MEI RELSA approved
Courses in English, Italian, Polish, Portuguese, Spanish, German and Japanese
Teacher training including CELT TEFL

Telephone: +353 (0) 91 566 468 Fax: +353 (0) 91 564 122
Email: info@galwaylanguage.com

Submissions for Crannóg 49 open July 1st until July 31st
Publication date is October 26th 2018

Crannóg is published three times a year in spring, summer and autumn.
Submission Times: Month of November for spring issue. Month of March for summer issue. Month of July for autumn issue.

We will <u>not read</u> submissions sent outside these times.

POETRY: *Send no more than three poems. Each poem should be under 50 lines.*
PROSE: *Send one story. Stories should be under 2,000 words.*

We do not accept postal submissions.

*When emailing your submission we require **three** things:*

1. *The text of your submission included both in body of email and as a Word attachment (this is to ensure correct layout. We may, however, change your layout to suit our publication).*
2. *A brief bio in the third person. Include this both in body and in attachment.*
3. *A postal address for contributor's copy in the event of publication.*

For full submission details, to learn more about Crannóg Magazine, to purchase copies of the current issue, or take out a subscription, log on to our website:

www.crannogmagazine.com

THE PIER

DAVID BUTLER

Ebbtide. Beneath the rhythmic slopping, ale-coloured waves lift lazy harbour detritus. Shrouds slap out-of-synch masts, a cantankerous tinkering. Above the car, gulls squabble psychotically.

A low hum has been diffracting all day through the slit to the top of the driver's window. A man who has not the air of paying the radio the slightest heed. A man who appears distracted, dishevelled, vaguely disreputable.

The ricochet steps of that woman with push-chair quickened just now as she pushed past, face forwards, eyes profiled. He hasn't seen her. Or if he has, her passage has made no more impression than the cavorting gulls.

His mind is elsewhere.

His mind is worn out.

Its cogitations whirr, gears gone in the teeth. He hasn't slept more than a catnap in days. Intractable, implacable insomnia has pushed a deep thumbprint beneath each eye. Fingers are nail-bitten and nicotine-stained. The jowl, coarse as sandpaper. Every so often the fingers flick open an empty cigarette box, shake it, toss it back onto the dashboard. It's hours since he smoked the last cigarette.

As far as the eye can see the sky is an estuary from which light is draining. He glances at the face of his wristwatch without reading it. All the while, like untutored metronomes, the masts beat irregular time.

*

'What were you thinking? I mean, what the fuck were you thinking?' Creegan's eyes, so pale beneath his glasses as to be almost transparent, had fixed on him furiously. No, not furiously. Willy Creegan could be many things, but not furious. He'd looked straight back at the thinning red hair, the outrage, the bristling moustache. 'What the hell were you thinking, Tom?'

Creegan looked around the bar, appealing for help, ensuring they were alone. 'Is she even seventeen?' After he'd hissed this question, this accusation, Will Creegan took a long draft from his pint that left a yellow tide-mark on the brush of his moustache. When no answer was forthcoming he'd sucked it clear. 'Seventeen.' His eyes widened, narrowed. 'Christ's sake!'

But Duffy had no answer. Not then, not now.

*

He fingers the cigarette box, tips out its vacancy, drops it onto the dashboard. With a will of its own it bounces, teeters, disappears somewhere to the far side of the gear stick. Seventeen! Duffy shuts his eyes, shakes his head, and groans.

He'd been suspended of course. As a matter of course. It wasn't that there'd been, ah, any suspicion of, ah, sexual misconduct ...

He pummels his forehead several times with the balls of his wrists. Oh by God there'd been suspicion all right, one should try to be, ah, precise about these things. Of course there'd been suspicion, Christ's sake!

The heels of his palms press slow circles into his sockets. Duffy can vividly see Janet Burke's moral brown eyes fixed rivet-like on his, her bosom inflated, her head elated with indignation. And the fierce muttering that died the instant he'd walked into the staffroom. I heard it wasn't ... 'twas too! A sixth-former? Go on! No, definitely. Who? No! One of them Poles is what so-and-so told me. It wasn't you-know-who, because ... And drunk, they say. There was a pair of them in it, so ...

Will Creegan, horrified, vulnerable, staring at him from behind the industrial coffee tin, the mug cradled, empty and impotent. All Duffy could do was shake his head to him as, one by one, his colleagues remembered a pressing duty to hurry them from the staffroom.

And then the egg-shaped head of McGrath, the, ah, principal, once he'd been summoned to the office. Tilted forwards, hand visor-like to forehead. So their eyes wouldn't meet. Who could tell what thoughts were hatching in that celibate crown? 'But, ah, Tom, I don't see, ah ... what exactly was the girl doing in your car, and, and ... and at that time of the evening?' A hiatus. 'Tom?'

Evening! It had been past midnight. A gloved hand that somehow belonged to that night's nightmare-logic had rapped, ruptured, interrupted abruptly at the window. Instantly Duffy was aware of the fug of whiskey sweetening the cigarette smoke. Instantly, of the schoolgirl who was curled on the passenger seat beside him. Magda Prokiewz, her eyes feral with alcohol, with anticipation. And the black, tactless glove tapped out a second time its peremptory Nevermore!

Duffy shakes his head. He sucks the stale air through incisors, breathes out, and pats the steering-wheel. From what Costello, the family lawyer, said on the phone, it doesn't look like he'll necessarily lose the licence. An irony there.

Will Creegan had said, oh years ago, that time he'd picked up the points for speeding, 'Did you know they refer to it as "endorsing" your licence? You'd imagine that'd be a good thing, having your licence endorsed. And by the Garda, no less.' Always the English teacher. For nigh on twenty years it was a part he'd played to the hilt, even when inside the staffroom. But for whose benefit? His own? No doubt his own. Creegan had never married. But he hardly believed in the role any more than the schoolkids did. It was some relic of his own schooldays maybe, the tweeds and the colourless sarcasm and the inordinate interest in words.

On balance, then, Duffy's licence mightn't be endorsed. True, after he'd blown a guilty lungful into the bag, after he'd stepped out of the car please sir, the urine sample he'd copiously provided down at the station had confirmed he was three times the legal limit. That much wasn't disputed. But when, officer? And where, officer? Had he been driving at all? Had they not consumed the whole damned naggin as they sat there in the car, he and his … underage companion? It was, at least, a possible scenario. And in the eyes of the law, in the eyes of the lawyer, possibility was what mattered.

Duffy shudders. Eight months ago (was it?), the time a tipsy Helen had skidded into the traffic lights, that was the very defence her paramour had had her mount. Was that the word? Doubtless Creegan would know! A man takes a mistress, but a woman? Whatever you'd call him, the very instant they'd punched into that traffic light, Silvio had hastened her into a bar that serendipity had placed directly facing the junction, where you could hardly miss it. They'd drunk off any number of shots as they waited for the guards to arrive. Dealing with the shock. Oh he was a cute whore, and no mistake.

*

'Why did you never get married, Will?'

To move the subject on, to get away from the indignity of revisiting his moment's madness. To break, at the least, the awful silence that had descended like a wall between the two teachers, he'd restrained his colleague's arm from lifting the pint a third time.

'Why do you ask that?'

'Come on, Creegan. Talk to me.'

The transparent eyes had lost none of their wounded indignation. But he was as reluctant as Duffy was to put twenty years' friendship through the trial of silence. He shrugged. 'Guess I never met the right gal.'

'Too easy.'

'What do you want me to say?' The tone had shifted. Already, Duffy sensed that Creegan was coming about, like a boat with its nose to the wind.

'You were going great guns with Dolores McIlroy for a while there.'

'Dolly!' Had he almost smiled? There was a faint twitch at the corners of the moustache, the tremble of a float that tells the lure is being tested. 'That's old history!' Was he punning, maybe? For seven years she'd taught history at their school.

'Before she moved on to Pres,' said Duffy, ostentatiously relaxing, 'most of the staffroom had the two of you hitched, I can tell you that. You heard of course she married their blond biology teacher up there, and he five years her junior? Rugby. D4, the whole package.' He chanced a wink. 'Someone even told me he's a Protestant.'

'I've always been of the opinion,' Creegan began to expostulate, donning his pedantry, he too relaxing, 'that's there's something inherently incestuous in the teaching profession. We never seem to marry outside the tribe.'

'Helen's no teacher.' The unexpected retort hung in the air. It surprised Duffy even more than Creegan.

'No, Tom, I'll grant you that.'

'No.'

'She was far too cute for chalk and talk, says you.' And suddenly, looking at the mild raillery in Will Creegan's face, Duffy had been gripped by a compulsion to confide in him. Memories welled up in him unchecked, like water throbbing in a fountain. And, caught in this unlooked for surge, his throat opened and closed, opened and closed. But words would not come.

How could he tell it?

How could he translate into language the gradual change of light that their marriage had been? That he imagined, finally, all marriages must be? This smug bachelor sitting across the table from him, Willy Creegan, who'd even been his best man, could he comprehend the sense of erosion? That underneath the giddiness of love, from the first, a tiny subsidence that each of them felt but never articulated? Resentment, was that it? If it was, it was aimed at the self as much as at the other.

No, it was impossible. Disappointment is intimate. And what word could ever represent the monstrous apathies and evasions, the silences that, with the years, swelled into tumours?

Or the shock of the first casual infidelity.

*

Helen would find out, of course. In due course. It was only a matter of time. For the present she doesn't even know that he's been suspended.

Duffy looks into the tentative dusk to where the sea beyond the harbour mouth is marbled like meat. The middle-aged men we used to laugh at, love, sitting in cars by the harbour, not getting out, not taking breeze or sun, covering their loneliness with newspaper, with radio, or staring vacant as mannequins at the moving water. Do you remember, love?

He tries out a laugh which transmutes into a cough.

What had he been thinking? Magda Prokiewz! A chance encounter, out by the park. Can I offer you a lift? Magda Magda

Prokiewz, high boots and cheekbones and oh so husky, seventeen going on twenty-seven. The guards hadn't even suspected till the duty sergeant asked her for her details. I'm sorry, you're how old?

Duffy gives a sour guffaw at the ignominy of it. Ignominy! There was a word that Creegan might use. Ignominious. Ignoble. Ignoramus.

The engine has thrummed into life. It seems his hand has turned the ignition.

All along the promenade street-lights are flickering on. From up on the Head they'll resemble a necklace. Far above the clamour, the seething tide, the jostle of masts. From where a car no bigger than a toy might be seen edging out onto the pier, how strange, what can it be doing? From where we watched the harbour lights come on, love. From where, the night of her nineteenth birthday, Duffy had proposed to her.

A PENTINA FOR MY LEOPARD COAT   KIM BRIDGFORD

I love everything about my old leopard coat:
Its style, its softness, and its vintage Calvin look.
(It made me buy another one, this year, in blond.)
It makes me strangely feel more loved, more desired,
As silly as that might sound. I feel like an animal.

One time, an owner, with an actual animal,
Told me that his dog was attracted to my coat.
For that reason – that my outerwear was desired –
The owner kept walking with me. Look, look,
He said. I did. The dog was beautiful and blond.

It happens everywhere. Bald, brunette, blond:
Nice coat! Sometimes they ask which animal,
And someone, once, complimented my hair, my look.
If you have a good haircut and a good coat,
What else matters? Laughed. Like a child desired,

I don't want to take off my coat. Leopard – desired
In my house – grew to pyjamas, another coat (blond),
A dress and jacket. It all comes back to my ur-coat.
Perhaps this is the reason I don't buy an animal:
Perhaps, one day, I am afraid that people won't look.

Sometimes, when I get my hair cut, to get my look,
My stylist laughs. She believes my coat story, desired
Along with my haircut. They think you're an animal.
No, no, I say. When I ask if I should be blond,
She says the same. No, no. It is that damned leopard coat.

Meanwhile, to be desired, I dream of the blond coat.
But I haven't worn it. It doesn't look like my spirit-animal.

NIGHT CYCLE ANDREW CALDICOTT

You aim for the high road
beyond town to burn off
the frustrations of the day.

There you will learn again
the hardest lesson of the road –
the hill will always beat you

if you allow it to come at you whole.
But if you break it down
stroke by stroke

it might surrender,
or at least allow you to pass
unvanquished.

But after, you must descend
into the shadow
of the trees

with only a thin beam of light
to guide you to the river
which will show you,

as it fades from silver
into the dusk,
releasing the night

sounds of the estuary,
how beauty is still
to be found,

And then to the sea road,
the long level of the shore
where you may become

rhythm,
cadence,
pulse.

Only then, when the world is turning
in the measure of your breath
and you know your heart

can lead you through movement,
through stillness,
through the dark,

should you return
to the clamour of streets
lit by the workings of other minds.

LITTLE POOLS OF LIGHT   SANDRA BUNTING

after Leonard Cohen

Sheep then leap to bring on sleep,
the fences are too high.
You shut your eyes and cease to weep,
a simple lullaby,

and on a dark and lonely breeze,
gliding bats begin to fright,
wild eyes look at you from trees.
Little pools of light.

The worm is hidden in the fruit,
crows stab with their beaks,
the apple sticks, makes them mute.
a circus act of freaks.

Back and forth the crash of waves,
decide what you can keep.
Chambered in the mind, it saves
in the place of good sleeps.

But what waits out in the forest dark
or through your inner sight,
by the sea or in the park?
Little pools of light.

Go deep down and meet the child
and ask it what it wants.
It's standing in a river mild,
frightened, small and gaunt.

Look at the one and take its hand.
You recognize its plight.
Walk with it in that murky land
to find little pools of light.

A BAD FIT   OLIVIA FITZSIMONS

The hot posh boy is shocked when I said I had a job at seven. Everyone did though. Where I'm from. I wasn't special. Luckier than most because my dad didn't piss his money away. Poor all the same because he made fuck all and it was the eighties with too many mouths to feed. But it could be today, things don't change much there.

Someone at the lovely party makes a joke about builders. We all laugh at my dad's job. I try not to say it among the children of the better ups but I'm contrary, can't help it. I've pretended I am one of them for so long but I'm just a cheap knock off. Hot boy considers me now like a collector as I reveal myself, a new exhibit from a vaudeville show and they crane their privileged necks to voyeurism. The exotic working class.

Poverty wouldn't look good on any of them. No matter how much they need it. The no, can't or won't rises up against agreeing to hug every opportunity yes like a skirt that's too short. I'll let him work a little harder for it. When everything is out of reach but you don't even know it. Back then we didn't notice, *not really*, because we had fresh air, freedom and ignored the grumblers. Or am I just kidding myself? So far removed that it seems safe to look back. We weren't the poorest. That was reserved for our neighbours a field away, more children than sense, a new one every year.

I smoke on the balcony listening to their voices lift and fall in the space of the five stars. I wonder aloud to no one why am I here. Some drunk tumbles red wine on an expensive gúna and its owner screams like the dead. I see my friend in the ground, brown dirt, gathering at pace on my snow-white dress I gave her. Pits of muck burrowing into the intricate lace, discolouring her tiny rigid arms, her battered hands within fingerless gloves forced together in an unanswered prayer. My holy communion dress. My gloves. My friend. Mine. My hand-me-down respectability for her.

I felt that twist in the stomach to me. I had desperately wanted to keep the bright milk-like silk dress heavy with crinoline, bunched satin drapes and intricate lace overlay all for myself. I had wanted the memory of trips to Tammy girl in the city choked with spring to buy spotted opaque virginal tights and *Gone with the Wind* gloves with matching parasol all for myself. I was sick of secondhand everything. I didn't want to share any of it. All by myself I was too young then to know that none of it was real, with nothing belonging to no one.

She had looked so pretty in it.

'That there dress sat in our closet,' my mother said, beatific, handing it over, 'sure it was only going to waste.'

Their dirty little faces piling out the door to stare at us, neighbours being neighbourly. How I cried in that wardrobe when it was gone. My mother left me to it. Her spoiled rotten daughter.

I didn't want to give it up, even if the words we said at mass were meaningless to me. Even if I was scared of the dark confession box smelling of incense, cocooning old white men with gruff voices who wanted to deliver my secrets up to a god who already failed me. A god who I had started to doubt.

When my tears dried my mother broke my heart all over again, said my rich posh aunt had bought the dress for me. She snarled words ashamed, my aunt a saviour, couldn't let the family down. Angry at me for something I could not comprehend. Poverty, don't say it out loud. Penance for a dying economy. Just push the pins in. For houses unbuilt and things laid down on hire purchase. Let the gypsophila crown run red with blood. So someone could look down on me. That sisters' lives could turn out so different.

The fairytale princess sits on the sofa covered in table salt, moaning gently as her suitors try to appease her. Long ago I realised this fable wasn't mine alone and shared it willingly then. Shared the pretence. Fantasy alive. Back then I told my friend the dress was borrowed too. That none of us owned it but for one day we could pretend. She smiled her big smile. Our grubby fingers pressed together. I've never felt as whole since.

After it happened I took the veil that I had hidden from my friend and gave it to her mother, who clawed at me and cried such sorrow sound it scared me half to death. Her raggedy older sister brought me out the back and slapped my face, then crying offered me a cigarette, my first nicotine hit, flying me coughingly high away from the small yard sadness.

I knew then someone has to be the worst. A name for it. Poor in the country is a different kind of terrible. I knew then we don't belong anywhere. Always on the outside. Leaving one place that you cannot stay for another that will never really love you. Your heart gets torn asunder so early on that it never knits itself back together. They found her in that dress, ripped and torn only a little, surprising they said given what took place. A trussed-up bride of christ, a poor trusting beautiful child.

I take the handsome boy home and try him on like a borrowed dress but nothing fits me anymore yet I pretend it looks good, I pretend he's mine. I'm so so good at pretending I even fool myself sometimes.

STAR ANISE JENNIFER WARING

Hold it

Between your fingertips
Broken carpelled

Touch your nose
To tender stelliform

Scent
the residue
of stale secretions

and liquorice dark
Potential.

Strain at the sound
of faint
cuspidate arms

fairy-belled
as they tip
against
the glass jar

Sky-patterned spices
miniature explosions
Burst in-stasis.

Slide your tongue
In between
Hard-edged
gaps

taste
their insides
Coaxed open
Labial
Unsatisfied.

THISTLECRACK   JANE BURN

Telephones are malevolent. Cradle-bones biding
until you have felt the evening's quietness spread
above the room and you, uneasy, try to settle below it.

Then, it will rack the air with shrill – you leap
from the chair, stub a toe in your hurry to answer. It slips,
soapy from your hands. This is how the complexities

of twilight pass. Dusk is easy to close the curtains against –
night comes like the healing of a wound. You close your door
upon it, shove the key down the throat of the lock, spin it dead.

Dawns keep coming – it has been your habit to rise to them.
Mornings you squat on the step, watching sun fledge
through the wall's topping of broken glass, edges tinkered

with glim. You know how jagged this place is. How it makes you
afraid. Policemen knock in a way peculiar to them –
their knuckles on wood say *something's wrong* and your heart

is all clatterbash in your chest. Tonight, they are door-to-door
after someone called about screams on nearby scrub. You say,
it's vixens make a noise like that but even as they go, slicing

the wasteland with knives of light, coining a fox's eyes with beams,
you lie in bed, headful of murder grasses and think how a pair
of arms would be a comfort. You live where you can afford to live –

most days, you just get on with it and dream of fields. Exist in
little things – see how fingers of spruce grasp invisible wind, how,
in a thistlecrack, petals feather from spiny bulbs, turn to down.

Step to avoid torched bins. When you live somewhere rough,
you can choose to hold sun in your eyes. Search out the trees.
Discover the best and worst of places look beautiful under snow.

WE ARE NOTHING BUT AFRAID — NATALIE CRICK

Our walls bear no stories.
An apple rests, dying.

Father counts the limp houseflies that
punctuate the sill.

Your tree, a fearless weed,
grows monstrous with leaves.
Bats hang like dark plums.

We're slumberous,
propped up by ghosts,
lips open and parched

repeating your name
about the house.
We hold death in our mouths.

THE RETURN OF HER   CLIVE DONOVAN

Still must a punctual goddess waken. David Gascoyne

She comes back trudging
Over desert edges

Thrusts her way through alleys
Between broken buildings

Her coat touching ground
A musky hint of verdant trail

On destroyed mortar delicate things
Start to creep

The bomb-shelled birds stir to sound again singing
And scarred trees weeping with raw new sap

Rising up she forces slabs and bricks
To accommodate such flowers as she chooses

The air softens and swells with charmed breezes
Channelled from the south

She lumbers and slouches oblivious and indifferent
To this sick charnel house we have made

Casts a cloak of worms over corpses
That once were frozen

She could take this whole fried city
– Smashed roads burnt patches tumbled girders

No match for her sweeping surge of seeds her countless
Nibbling mulching creatures – we too if we wish

Could strip off armour and uniform
Breathe in rich aromas of earth and green grass of

Her skirt as she strides by welcoming and worshipping her
– Spring – Persephone! – cleansing everything.

LOOK AND SEE   SHEILA GORMAN

My name is Faith. I used to have some, faith that is. In myself. In my surroundings. But not any more.

I like my room. I know what's in here. An iron bed (the cream paint's a bit chipped), a table and a small wardrobe. Scrubbed floorboards, two windows. I don't need much.

I use old jam-jars for my paint brushes and a small oblong wooden box with a sliding lid for my pencils. I have an old wicker picnic basket for the bottles of ink and tubes of paint. People here give me paper – watercolour paper sometimes. But mostly I use scraps, brown bags or even newspaper.

I don't let them come in though. People. They say I have the only key. I keep the door locked. I dust and sweep. No one can disturb me. It is my room after all.

I like to wet the paper and watch as the inks and paints soak and leach into one another. I like to see which absorbs the other. Which colour wins. I write some words.

Some days I look closely at my pinned dragonflies. They are such beautiful creatures. The light catches their wings. Their iridescent bodies glint behind the glass. Unfortunately, their colour fades on death. In life, they rely almost completely on their sight. Their eyes make up two thirds of their heads and they have all-round vision. Little escapes them.

I was thinking of making a list of the things in my room. Windows. Bed. Table. Paint brushes. Picnic basket. Dragonflies. Everything. If it wasn't on the list and I saw it, then I'd know it wasn't really here. Wouldn't I? If I was in doubt about something I saw I could check the list. Then I'd know.

Lately it has become even more difficult to tell if what I see is actually happening here beside me or somewhere else altogether. So I made that list. Now I cross things off when I take them out. Add things when I bring them in or if I get new ones.

It's when I leave my room that the real trouble starts. I've no list then. If I walk down the corridor, I should know what to expect. Shouldn't I? Don't you? A mountain would be unrealistic in a corridor, or a lion or zebra. But a person would not be unexpected. Most people could be there. Not soldiers, that's true, but ordinary people, even firefighters, would be a possibility. Are they there, before my eyes in the corridor, behind my eyes in my head or are they somewhere else altogether? I once hoped that my drawings would help me tell the difference between what is real and what is not. They don't. I continue to make them though the drawings prove nothing.

The zebra. Of course, even without my list, I know they can't be in my room. At first my view is blurred. Golden vertical lines become stems of grass that begin to move in the breeze. A baby zebra totters on the dappled savannah and finds its mother in the herd. It recognises her by the arrangement of her stripes. Suddenly something startles them and they're all on the move. Earth dust. The sun highlights the grass as the zebra slow. They stop and drop their heads to graze.

The sun shines and the grasses are bending in the wind. An adult zebra raises its head quickly in alarm. A lion's head appears just above the top of the grass. The whole herd starts moving again. Panicking. I can see that the single baby zebra on its long spindly legs is being left behind. The lion spots the straggler, runs towards it. The creature is zigzagging, trying to escape. The lion is jinking. It leaps, claws out. The fallen zebra kicks. The herd stops a little way off. They don't understand. Stepping outside the herd can be dangerous.

The zebra cannot be in the room with me. So when I see it, I know that it's not here. Nor is the grass. Nor the lion. Not really. But if they are not here, where are they?

I wait for my blood to be taken. They say it's to see if I am getting better but I don't believe them. Could be for anything. Perhaps they're making a collection of it to sell or to inject into another body. Who's to say? They don't seem interested in testing my eyes, nor my vision.

The small zebra is only bones now. Its black and white hide lies hollow. I load my brush with water and drench my drawing of the animal. I like painting into wet paper and watching the colours move. Chance mixings happen. I like to allow for the chance of flow. I draw. I paint. I dip another brush into the red ink and drop it onto the page. The red bleeds and eddys.

Sometimes I paint half a grapefruit, an orange or a flower. It is amazing what I can see when I really look. Not assume what is there but see it as it is. I study it for a good stretch of time before I start. I see the shadows and the spaces, the details of what makes it what it is. Once I can see it, observe it, I can draw it. I see the cut fruit and the juice as it dribbles down the skin.

There are cameras in the grounds here. Most are focused on the perimeter fence and on some of the more vulnerable entries and exits. I always try to avoid being seen so I have a special route I take for my walks. I prefer to remain out of range. But I know that orbiting satellites can take pictures of even a coin on the pavement. They can see me too but probably only the top of my head, my shoulders and maybe my toes sometimes.

When I'm out I can be walking, keeping my eyes down, just following the rhythm of my feet. If I see something move, even out of the corner of my eye, I stop. Perhaps my stillness will mean that no one can see me. Some animals are like that. They see only movement. A static figure blends invisibly into its surroundings. Sometimes what I see is as close as my eyelashes. Sometimes what I see is in the distance. Sometimes it is not truly there.

I have asked them to install a mirror opposite the peep hole in my door so that I can check if anyone is coming before I leave my room. But how do I tell if someone is going to come out of their room, or be along the corridor when I am already out there?

I'm glad that no one can see into my room. No one can tell my hair is accumulating in my hairbrush or look at my reflection in the mirror. They can't glance at the toothpaste drying on the side of my hand-basin or be revolted by the dry skin as it flakes off my legs when I take down my stockings. They can't watch the dust falling and gathering under my bed.

Ideally, I would live alone in a big house with lots of rooms. The light would come in and move around at its own pace. But as things are, I've decided to stay in my room. I know what's in here. Two windows. A bed, a table, a small wardrobe, dragonflies. I don't need much. I use old jam-jars for my paintbrushes and a small wooden box for my pencils. They're all on my list.

Suddenly in the display case the dragonflies beat their wings frantically. The glass cracks. Splits. Shards fly embedding themselves into my floor. It has become impossible to tell what is true and what is false, what is imagined and what is real. The list doesn't help.

My name is Faith. I used to have some, faith that is. In myself. In my surroundings. But not any more.

AMONG THE LIVING   A. MAHLON REECE

for Bret Anthony Johnston

1.
I knelt for one hour on one knee
reading Anne Sexton
trying to find the lines where she reveals
the reasons why
some of us want to die all the time.

I like you, Anne. You say that death begins
like a dream
with loved one's laughter
and wild blueberries,
where the dead refuse to be blessed,
men kill to be touched,
and love's an infection.

Anne, prophetess of destruction,
I'm still among the living.
Anne, with your dark truth
and old dwarf heart,
I love you.

Wrap your poisoned arms around me.
I am lonely, too.

2.
My best friend of ten years
called me from the psychiatric hospital.
Her voice was very small and thin
like the powder-white almond blossoms
on that Van Gogh print
we bought in Amsterdam those years ago
when we were married.

Such branched loveliness –
it made her very happy then.

Pain is hard to uproot: so vast,
a splendour of ruin.

3.
Practise death, Plato says,
because we're out of tune,
drunk with lust and ignorance
flying our fleshy chariots
into the sun until we burn
and the centre of our firework
goes CRACK
and somebody says, 'Awww – how beautiful'
or 'what a shame'

and only dark and smoke remain.

WHO SENT YOU?   HONOR DUFF

In pain and feeling my crabbéd age, annoyed
that some bad goblin of the supermarket trolleys
had made me pick the one with a wonky wheel,
I entered the store, wincing at the unrelenting glare
of lights, noting the same display of weary flowers,
helpless immigrants, needing water and rescue.

With scowling face and head well bent, I hoped
not to encounter anyone I'd have to greet,
paste a rictus smile on my face, swop banalities
about the weather or the heavy traffic in town.

I saw her from the corner of my jaundiced eye,
a little girl with fairytale new-minted golden hair.
She held her father's hand, bestowed a smile
of such sweet radiance that I stood still,
wondered could such a gift be meant for me,
was she not scared of my Medusa face?
But, there was no-one else nearby, so I smiled back,
and as she left, imagined I saw downy feathers float.

AN ODE SPINS THROUGH THE NIGHT SADDIQ DZUKOGI

From the moment I felt your fingers streel through the foot of my memory, I began to believe in ghosts. I ask where is the abyss: my wound sizzles, an ode spins through the night like an injured coyote howling at the hollow-spaces. I lean further into my loneliness, each time sorrow pushes my body off a cliff, every word shaken off their meaning like drenched dogs. What do the ears of the dead hear when the incus is shaken out of place? I no longer have a name, since the cold-flame of death touched your shoes and swallowed all the places you're meant to be. I could see myself pick up your wrist as you unfurl into a wildwood where the sky is enveloped with ravines and its dentures caught in the silhouette of rain clouds. My child, do you mind my asking what you did with your body? I can't feel your limbs the way I used to feel them – the lamppost shows the way you sloughed off your skin – the headstone secures its presence. I won't go into details because my shadows make the mark on your grave, a dreamy space filled with lily-leaves that deprive me of my dreams.

EARWORM ÓRLA FAY

after 'Better Love' by Hozier

The words and melody slip into my mind
on repeat, their emotion an anchor
that drops down to an ocean
where you are swimming
glittering and green
mermaid-like.
And the blue of the depths is as blue
as the teal of the falling sky
uplifted at sunset.
Yahweh do angels walk among us,
whispering such lyrics
as catalyst?
What it must be to cup a beating heart
in hand, or a bird or 21 grams,
to travel through time,
to scale the wall,
to rise again
after the fall?
How could I be deceived by what is fake,
the shaded figure that stands
in shadows without colour,
without truth or fire
in cowardice?

But now this brainworm, this sticky music
sees me suffer stuck song syndrome,
amazes me with the imagery
of fire weeping from cedar,
teaches me calque;
the lent word
ohrwurm, earworm,

the meaning of.

NIGHT CYCLE — MARY ELLEN FEAN

For the lost children at Tuam

It was another famine, a starvation
of love and mercy —
In this time, a father sets his
daughter on the bar of a bicycle
twenty weeks pregnant and
husbandless, banished from her
people, beyond redemption.

Setting out by night, the next town
is a safe enough distance, a secret to
be kept. An empty road, a fox looks out,
he cannot tell, he feels the heat of her
head against his cheek, as when she was
a little girl, on this same bike.

The nuns would be kind to them, his only
daughter and her child, the winter grazing
on the curate's field is the weight of his
bargain.

Hydrangeas bloom in the convent garden,
cornflower blue, purest white, he sets her
down, his foot on the gravel for balance
her face is a window without a light.

TEARDROPS MARTIN KEAVENEY

The dog had been missing since morning. It was getting late in the day, but I still wasn't too keen on going home to dad at the dinner table to tell him there was no sign of Del Boy and we'd have to put an ad out on local radio.

I'd been asking at the houses on the boreen where Del Boy had gone off on his travels. There was only one place left, and I'd kind of hoped I wouldn't have to call in there.

We'd been moving a few bullocks from one parcel of land to another that morning. I liked shifting stock along the side road; it was partly shaded with high beech trees that hung across in places, like you were in a tunnel. There was a nice smell of pine trees from the wood about half way. There'd be a cool rhythm from the cattle's pounding hooves as they scuttled along, Del Boy snapping at their heels. All you had to do was ignore the plop-plop-plop of steaming green shite, the sudden pools of frothy piss. Del Boy had been hunting them along nicely and next thing he was gone. I didn't take much notice for a while; he'd often nip off, chasing down a stoat or a hare in the long summer hay grass. It was like he always knew when something was happening, like he was drawn to it. But by the time we got back to the main road, there was still no sign and dad was rearing up.

It wasn't that I was afraid of the Fadgins. I'd never seen any of them. I'd heard there was just a couple of old lads living there. I wasn't sure if they were brothers or father and son, I never got around to asking dad.

I knew they were more than likely harmless, and it was probably the whole look of the place that gave me the shivers. It was a yellow pebble dashed cottage, amongst a thick crowd of fir trees, with two red tiled bay windows at the front, always curtained across, a sure sign of men in bed during the day, we knew. There was a curly chimney cowl in the centre of the roof, with shamrock stamped ridge tiles either side, a ribbon effect fascia board along the top of the wall. The little lawn had a cracked concrete path, and there were all these small white statues, dad said they were meant to be mythical Greek gods, figures that were supposed to rule things like love, war and death. But they all looked the same to me. There was a big gate clad with red galvanised sheets to the side. It was always closed, and I used wonder what they had behind it. They had pheasants that would be chortling as we'd pass. You usually didn't see them, but you'd hear them too well, they'd make you shiver, and the cattle would be pure disturbed. One time, I saw one in the garden on the cracked path. It was hissing and had spread out a massive fan of blue, green and red feathers amongst the gods.

I parked the bike at a low wall made of hourglass-shaped concrete moulds, painted white and yellow. It took a bit of shuffling to pull back the bolt on the little red gate, flakes of rust fell on the grass. The path slabs lifted and clicked under my boot fall as I went up to the front door.

I knocked and waited for a few minutes. It was dead quiet, and I was just turning back to the boreen when the door opened.

Mickey Fadgin stared out. He wore a grey shirt over trousers held together with a half-looped belt. He had a coat of stubble, and he was barefoot.

'Hey?'

'How ya, Mickey. I was just looking for our old dog. You didn't see him?'

'Who are ye?'

'John Henry's son. We were bringing a few cattle down the way this morning. I haven't seen him since.'

Fadgin nodded slowly and stared.

'That's alright so,' I said, the path slabs clicking.

'Come,' Fadgin said. He went down the hall and left the door open. I stepped across a faded 'Merry Christmas' mat and shut the door.

It was hard to see in the hall; a door was open into the front room to the right, where a bit of the day was coming through the curtains. Most of the light was from an end door which led into a small kitchen.

When I went down there, I saw Del Boy under a long table. He ran out, jumped up on me, panting, thick paws on my chest.

'Hey, boy, where'd you get to?' I rubbed the top of his head.

'He was at the door this morning, scratching. I heard the hooves down the road alright, but I thought it was just a stray. He was whining.'

Del Boy was still whining a bit.

'What's wrong, boy? What's on ya?' I looked into his black eyes. They blinked back.

Fadgin had leant against a smoky Stanley range. All the tiles had fallen away behind; there were just combed clouds of blackened tiling grout. Then I saw a man at the other end. He was a good bit older than Fadgin. He was sitting back in the chair, hands flat on the table, eyes shut tight.

'That's alright so. I better be going.'
'Will ye have a drop of something?'
'No, it's alright.'
'Have a small one, for Christ's sake!'

I went over to the near end of the table. Fadgin clapped. Del Boy went back under the table, laid his head on his thick front paws. The only sounds for a few moments were his panting and low whining.

I pulled out a chair; the feet scraped on the concrete where the lino stopped. Fadgin was across at a tall dresser. It had glass panelled doors on top. There were decorated blue plates on their end along the back of the top shelf, small teacups with the same design on saucers across the front. Everything looked fairly dusty. Fadgin went to one of the presses at the bottom. The door squeaked open. Inside, the shelves were covered in newspaper. He pulled out a bottle of Jameson and three fancy glasses. He came over and put the glasses out, opened the bottle and filled each to a third.

'Drop of water?' He nodded to the square white sink in the corner behind me.

'No, it's grand.'
'Neat so.'

He pushed the glass to me and another down to the old man.

'Good luck.' Fadgin drank his down and put the glass back on the table with a bang.

I sipped mine. It stung my throat.
'What class are ye in?'
'Second year.'

'What?' Fadgin's eyes squinted.
'Second year. In secondary school.'
'Ah. That's alright. Do ye want another?'
'No, thanks.'
'Drink up then. Will ye have a smoke?'
'No, thanks.'

Fadgin pulled out a green box of cigarettes from somewhere. He lit up; the smell filled the room.

I sipped the whiskey again, my eyes watered, my cheeks got hot.

'Do ye play cards?'
'Sometimes. At school.'

Fadgin drew on the fag and left it on the edge of the table. He clapped and went back to the dresser. I looked at the fag burning away and then down the table to the old man. His drink was untouched.

Fadgin reached far into the press and pulled out a battered USA biscuit tin. He brought the tin over and fiddled for a minute with the lid. When it came off, he put the fag in his mouth, smoke clouds curving around his head, and took out a rosary beads, a comb, a thick roll of cash, a couple of big batteries, a rusty-looking penknife and, after he'd moved a lot of other things around, a worn pack of playing cards, held together with a thick elastic band.

'Ye can play "25"?'

I nodded and drank a bit more of the whiskey. Fadgin tossed the fag butt onto the range hot plate and shuffled the pack. I thought I'd just get up and go, say nothing more and walk out with Del Boy, yet still I took the hand he dealt.

We played a couple of tricks. I won both.

'You're fair handy.'
'Lucky.'
'It's how ye play the luck.'

Fadgin clapped. He threw everything into the tin again and fixed on the lid. He gathered up the three glasses, the bottle and put the lot back in the press.

I stood up.

'I better be going.'

'Do ye like music?' Fadgin said, as he came back to the table.

'It's alright.'

'Come.'

Fadgin went into the hall. I followed, Del Boy behind me. Fadgin had gone straight into the front room. There was a weird light in there through the curtains; it made everything seem red. The carpet was thick and there was a pair of armchairs and a settee covered with sheets. The room was decorated with flowery wallpaper and there was a smell of damp.

Fadgin pulled a sheet off one of the armchairs, a floorboard creaked under his movement.

'Sit.'

I sunk into the seat opposite a small empty marble fireplace. Del Boy made himself comfortable on the carpet, head on paws. Even though it was roasting outside, the room was cold.

Fadgin was at the far wall. I thought he was opening up more presses, but it was the lid of a piano. He pulled out a stool from underneath. He sat and tapped a few of the keys. They didn't sound right, like they were out of tune.

He turned back to me and clapped. 'It'll be alright.'

Then he played for a good while. I didn't know the melody. Del Boy's tail started twitching. The hairs lifted on the back of my neck about halfway through. Maybe it was the whiskey, but toward the end, my eyes started watering. I was shaking all over. Fadgin was going up and down the keys so fast, as if he was electrified and it felt a bit like when I'd touch an electric fence at the silage pit with a blade of grass, and you could stand there, in the middle of winter, while the cattle munched at the feeder, and you'd be getting all these little jolts of voltage.

It was like Fadgin could hit all the keys at once, or that there were loads of pianos, all playing at the same time, like it was some kind of massive concert in the tiny red room. I sat forward, teardrops fell onto the carpet. Del Boy looked at them and sniffed, and then it was as if we weren't even there any more, the whole lot, me, Fadgin and Del Boy had been lifted up out of there, now we were lost, gone out of the boreen, to some other way different place.

When Fadgin stopped playing, Del Boy looked up. It was pure silent in the front room.

'You can make it sing,' I said.

Fadgin clapped and smiled.

'This was the aunt's. She had us tormented to learn it when we were small. We –'

There was a bang in the kitchen. Fadgin looked at the wall. He got off the stool.

I followed him out and stood at the door to the kitchen. Fadgin pulled the old man's head up from the table and set him back into the chair.

'Thanks for the drink, Mickey.'

Fadgin didn't look at me. He leant against the Stanley, watching the old man.

It took ages to find the latch for the front door in the darkness. My hand kept hitting against some soft furry thing hanging from the ceiling. When the light finally flashed into the hall, I saw it was a long strip of flypaper, the yellow sticky tape covered in hundreds of decomposing insects.

I WAS GIVEN — MARY MELVIN GEOGHEGAN

in the hospital
after your name was called
you caught my heart.
Through the hospital door
through the pouring rain
almost, as if you were still with me.

Passing time –
in the Hugh Lane Gallery
round the corner from the hotel.
Sean Scully's waiting –
dragging me across his canvases
out beyond all form and line.
But, upstairs there's more
Francis Bacon speaking directly to camera
revealing how accidentally he discovered
the back of the canvas worked better for him.
How, out of necessity
he was given.

AUGUST IN MEMORIAM   CAITLYN ROOKE

Hands, chilled with day's close, comb through silted locks while
the decades worn towel wrapped around falls to sand-dusted toes.
Pruned fingertips check the elastic round my waist as I leave
fire's confines, throwing warmth over for the motion of stillness.

I hop from soft to soft above smooth stones, slowing only as toes taste
water's ebb. I don't linger on his not quite scattered ashes in the
shallows.
But I note their fine white paleness against the coarse ochres
of our shore, a transient monument for the ashes which still glow.

I cut around this life under glass and into the water until the rounded
part of my belly sits below the line and I imagine I'm slim like sixteen.
I know I'll go under but I don't think of it as I slip down. Eyelids resting
together, I know light and dark by their coldness and warmth.

And with arced back I rise to see the sun's belly on the line,
its pinkness blooming into the water with no thought.

PRINCIPLES OF FATHERHOOD — KEVIN GRAHAM

Ducking into the flowery concrete tube we like to try our voices on
and listen for something in them, an echo of what it means
to be alive. In the bath he shivers at the anointing water, eyes
wide with shock that breath can leave so naturally. My hands clasp
his bloody knee as I play Buddha to his currency of pain.
The tide rolls in and moonlight plays in the everlasting sky.

*

His chin wobbles because the toy boat he's clutched all day
is missing. I remember the ultrasound, how for days I couldn't
turn off his deafening heartbeat. Among the things to forget
is staring above his head where a lark's nest jammed
between branches is falling apart. Signals come and go – a man
with one arm in the bin, a field of daisies pushing up the sun.

*

I'm tying bunting in the garden, breaking cobwebs laced
to leaves. A cake's been bought, goodies dropped in paper bags,
each place laid with deferential care. When they come it's horseplay
and chatter, screams of laughter. I catch him in the cardboard
spaceship that's been launched on the patio, apex teetering.
We huddle together like Neanderthals, share a precious breath.

*

The playground's ours at this hour. He slides out of my arms
and makes his way to a red and yellow tractor. Then it's
the swing and this morning's brief amnesia, our two lives
hanging in the balance. The trees are breezy and we make fake tea
in a wooden hollow. I ignore the wonky swastika on the ceiling,
focus instead on the important thing he's trying to say.

*

We're running after rain, the ground pulling away inch by anxious inch. He shakes his head as if to dislodge a bee trapped in his skull. Birdsong on a limb, the world faint with pain. Holding a stick in his grubby paw, dust settles in the middle distance. Where is he going? How far? I follow in his footsteps, watch him part the brightening air.

SO I DIDN'T STAY 'TIL THE END — S. K. GROUT

Stuck inside a whole lot of love,
that you can't ignore. Here is my heart.
I give you all, even though it's broken
bent out of shape, disorderly. The frozen
winter lake offers a chance of half
fun, half fear. I just look out.

Winter shortens the days, I'm running out
of time. All the preparations find the love,
loss and lesser things, bit by bit, half
happiness, some dread. A baby deer heart
cramps black on the porch; its body frozen
by the cold, and the predator's maw, broken

the body snapped in two, not bullet-broken.
Taken, instead, by nature's cycle. I want to love
you, I think, but I just can't see it out.
Follow the love – but what if your heart
can't be trusted? What if it's a frozen
piece of rock inside you semi-alive, half

vanishing? What if you don't want to eat my half
of the meal? What if you won't see yourself out?
When you woke up, the bed was already broken.
You need to bury the dead deer, love.
You need to cut it up because it won't all fit, heart
first in some kind of ritual, that is time-frozen.

It's stinking out the porch, despite the frozen
slippery floor. Some stranger will arrive, broken
knees or legs or arms and complain, in some half
witted way about our lack. You need to clean out
the dead deer, you need to cut it up and give it some love,
even in death. Maybe it knew how to use its heart.

I'll make something out of wood, a carved heart
while you work. I'm whittling away one half
already laid in front of the fire, starting from frozen.
This will become precious and good and not broken.
You take away the dead deer, clear the mess out.
I'll carve a word on this heart. What shall it say? Love?

The answer to my frozen prayer was to follow love
out of here: broken bones, things, beds mean nothing
in the half-light. I know. But, my heart beats treachery.

THE BEACH AT YOUGHAL   EDEL HANLEY

There's a black ribbon road that brings us home
On the way back from the beach at Youghal.
It always reminds me of you,
And how you used to love it there, at my age.

We held hands down by the water during those summers
And ate ham sandwiches by the rocks.
Do you remember that day when I found the dead crab
Under a dry heap of washed up seaweed

Where we sat, side by side?
The fat gulls mewed, nonchalant,
Overhead,
And melted ice-cream smeared across your denim skirt.

You carried my small, red bucket in your left hand
As we walked to the shore,
And we built sand castles
Until the night swept in, gentle, and always too soon.

STUDY IN CHARCOAL   TAMZIN MITCHELL

Irene left her suicide note on Instagram: train tracks stretching into the prairie against a tired blue sky. Noon train to nowhere. #saskatchewan #greatplains #traintracks #sorry #theend. She posted it, turned off her phone, and set off down the tracks, one rail tie at a time.

*

Jake picked her up at the hospital on Monday, after her mandatory seventy-two-hour hold. After she convinced the psychologists and psychiatrists and nurses that she wasn't an immediate danger to herself. Her hospital roommate had been a harder sell, but she'd thought she was Saint Rita, patron saint of impossible causes, so Irene had given herself partial points. Irene had spent most of the weekend curled on a couch in the too-cold common room, wearing a thin white hospital gown over grubby jeans, her hands wrapped around tepid Styrofoam cups of decaf coffee. Psych-ward patients weren't to be trusted with boiling water, china, or caffeine.

'Jesus, Irene,' Jake said as she closed the passenger door of his clunker. Their clunker, he always said, but since he needed it for his work as a claims adjustor, only he drove it. 'What were you thinking?' Although she didn't turn to face him, she could feel his look of exasperation. 'Instagram? That's so ... millennial.'

Against her better judgment, she laughed. 'Hashtag "no excuse,"' she said drily.

He relaxed a little and turned the key in the ignition. 'Okay,' he said.

A few minutes later, as they trundled over the South Saskatchewan River, she stretched, felt her lank brown hair, and grimaced.

'What?' Jake said, glancing between her and the bridge. 'Did they not give you shampoo or something?'

'I wasn't going to shower with people watching,' Irene said. 'No – for fuck's sake, Jacob. Don't look at me like that. Real people. Nurses. To make sure you don't off yourself in the shower.'

If she'd aimed to shock him, it hadn't worked. The car kept its steady pace, and Jake just sighed. But then he dug into his jeans pocket, lifting his hips slightly to get a better angle, and reached out to her. 'Here,' he said. 'You left this on the bathroom counter.'

Her ring. Her not-an-engagement-ring ring. Her Claddagh ring, a crowned heart held gently in two hands. Jake had given it to her when they moved in together, saying it was in honour of their shared Irish heritage. He hadn't used the word 'love', and he'd assured her that he wasn't ready to think about marriage, but he'd said it was white gold, bought when he'd backpacked around Europe a few years before they'd met. 'You wear the heart pointing out to show that you're in a relationship,' he'd said, slipping it on the middle finger of her right hand. Her skin had turned an unhealthy-looking green under the ring, which she was pretty sure didn't happen with white gold, but she just scrubbed the stain off with nail-polish remover every so often and let Jake keep his fiction.

'Thanks,' she said now. She slid it back on her finger – currently unstained – and touched the point of the heart. The end of the bridge loomed, and Jake was looking at her again. 'What?' she said flatly.

'You knew that railroad is mostly disused, right?' he said. 'That there aren't any trains there on Fridays?'

She shrugged noncommittally. She hadn't known, but she thought she might have done the same thing anyway. 'Oh,' she said. 'Hey. Can you drop me at the studio?'

'You don't want to shower first?' he asked. 'I have to go back to the office for a while, but I thought we could talk later.' He didn't mean it, she thought; if he'd wanted to talk, he would have visited during her psych hold.

'I'll have to shower after the studio anyway,' Irene pointed out. Clay got everywhere, working its way into the seams of her jeans and deep under her fingernails. 'I'll, like, fire you a mug or something.' She'd brought home at least a dozen by now, cramming them into a tiny cupboard in their cluttered kitchen, although Jake only drank coffee that came in paper Starbucks cups.

'How hipster,' Jake muttered, but he threw a glance over his shoulder and spun the steering wheel abruptly left, toward the studio.

*

When Irene had dropped out of her master's program at the University of Saskatchewan sixteen months earlier, her mother had told her to come home to Vancouver – to civilisation – and do something practical. 'We left Saskatchewan so that we'd never have to live through another prairie winter,' she'd said. 'I don't know what you're trying to prove.' But Irene liked the way her cheeks tingled as wind whipped through barren trees in winter and the way the radiators clanked and belched. There had been enough to keep her here, at least for a while, and she hadn't gone home. Instead she had moved into Jake's grimy one-bedroom and flitted between waitressing jobs until the Saskatchewan Arts Council had awarded her a year-long grant, one that came with studio space and just enough money to keep her in groceries and art supplies. The grant was almost over, and she and Jake hadn't talked about what came next.

A dried-out hunk of clay sat forlornly on Irene's pottery wheel, and she scraped it off, wet her hands at her pocket-sized sink, and began anew. Her fingers dug easily into the slick, grainy material, shaping it automatically, idly. She'd gotten the arts grant on the basis of her portfolio of charcoal sketches – helped or hindered by the fact that she'd written her application in charcoal on graph paper, she wasn't sure – but she'd spent the first cheque on a portable pottery wheel and since then had done nothing but throw misshapen vases and zigzagging mugs that were sharp-edged but perfectly centred. When she glazed them in earth tones, Jake called them hippie, and when she etched homicidal unicorns into the sides, he called them hipster. Today she thought she'd etch a penny-farthing on the side of a mug and glaze it in umber and mossy green to see whether 'hipster' or 'hippie' would prevail.

'Where were you this weekend?' Irene's next-door neighbour, Lucian, was leaning in through her open doorway, cradling a thin, half-full china cup. Or half empty, Irene supposed, but with Lucian it was probably half full. Like Irene, he'd grown up in Saskatoon, but unlike Irene, who'd left and come back, he'd simply never bothered to leave. She should offer him a better mug, purple to match his paint-stained nails. He'd gotten his arts grant for an intricately detailed graphic novel, its story told without words, but these days he hurled blobs of paint at canvases and let the colours run together. When they were both in a groove, Irene thought the whir-thump of her wheel and his paint made an art-studio-specific sort of music.

'Locked up in a psych ward,' she said evenly.

Lucian laughed. 'Well, that would be a way to find inspiration,' he said, but whether or not he thought she was kidding, he didn't press for details. He straightened and moved closer to inspect her progress. 'Huh,' he said, not quite touching a long, fluid indentation in the clay. 'That's a kind of cool effect. From your ring?'

Irene looked down to see that she'd forgotten to take off the Claddagh ring, which was now encrusted with a thick layer of clay. She usually left it at the apartment. 'Oh,' she said, wiping off some of the excess. 'Oops.'

'No, it's cool,' Lucian said again. He squinted at her hand. 'Wait, did you finally dump Jake? It's about time. You need to date an artist. Not me,' he added in response to Irene's raised eyebrow. 'But someone who creates things other than claims assessments. Jake thinks having been to Europe once makes him interesting.'

'What the fuck, Lucian,' Irene said. 'No. We didn't break up. Why?'

'Your ring is on the wrong way,' Lucian said.

'No, it's right,' Irene said. 'Pointing away. For romance, or something like that.'

Lucian pulled out his phone and thumbed open a web app. 'The Internet here sucks,' he said. 'But look. See? It's supposed to be toward you if you're in a relationship.'

Irene stared at the screen, resisting the urge to take it in her ochre-stained hands. It seemed suddenly fitting: not even a cheap representation of a relationship but a cheap representation of a non-relationship. 'How about that,' she said.

*

Irene left her break-up letter on the bed, in the form of a charcoal sketch: a hand wearing a Claddagh ring, heart split down the centre and pointed toward the body. How artsy, she wrote on the middle finger. She signed it Dear John, putting a big flourish on the J, packed her pottery wheel into its wheeled crate and cushioned it with her filthy studio clothes, and set off for the train station, one step at a time.

THE SKY CONFESSES — MARK HART

My innocent blue – that's only a ruse.
I am a mirage
over the abyss of the heavens.

It's my job to make the earth
seem cosy. I make the sun seem
to reign alone. He's jealous
and needs to believe in
a monotheism of himself.

You understand, of course.
You're an old hand at making
bargains with the truth. Daily
you replace your unknowable soul
with a sunny personality.

Night comes, the sun leaves,
and I roll my blue back like an awning.
The boundaries of your little world bleed
into the darkness thickening around you.
You feel naked, missing my cover.
Or small, lost in the vastness.
Missing my ceiling, you seek your hole,
turn on the lights. Perhaps you allow yourself
a little awe before you go in.

STANDING PEOPLE ANDREA WARD

For Fionnuala

The blackbird and, oh, chaffinch and now
robin sing nesting, sing the May sun
filtering dapples to the few ferns
unfurling and the bluebells spring-tiding
through colonnades of beech.
Hoverflies stitch light zig-zag to light.
The air breathes yellow-greening
and billows tenderly the first limp leaflings

– downy they are, you tell me, like babies,
like my youngest, nested and unpleating
on my back that summer while I raked
and stooped, picking stones, always
rooting in the earth that the builders
had left sloping from the banked up lawn.
The cedar was there already on the boundary, with
sycamores, where the children rigged a tree house.

I had a calendar picture, you tell me,
of sunlight through beech trees. I dreamed
of living in woodland. Just a pound each
I bought them for. Two and a half feet high,
they were. Mostly beech – and three oaks
and two Spanish chestnuts. It was autumn
when I sowed them in narrowing rows
 – trompe d'oeil – towards the shine of the river.

*In this soil twenty-six years, you answer, and indeed
tall for their age. A law unto themselves.
Standing People, the Cherokee would call them.
They had to power up, so closely planted, under-
and overground enmeshed completely. And anyway,
the undepleted earth is generous. The rush
of oxygen from the first leaves is like spring water:
a homing draught to stay us in our standing.*

IF IT IS TRUE THAT HUMANS ARE MOBILE TREES
DEIRDRE HINES

there is a hidden music in
                    rain drumming rittle rattle through leaves
each tree
                    that breaks from earth
is melody of wingthrum
                    opening our imagos
to beehum
                    wings that sense the way
by frogchorus
                    are magnetoceptic
and thunderous
                    jaguar roar
carries us deep into
                    fog forests to sing
worlds into being
                    with the U'wa
Spectacled Bear
                    Manoba
chases us across
                    the skywalk
below hanging bridges
                    giggles of water
wake us to sip
                    from dracula simia orchids
in orange scented shafts
                    beside a road
block
                    tree sit-in platforms
unite us
                    sing to the leaflight
in our veins.

TORN   PAMELA JOHNSON

I can't believe it's him – thumb-sized
yet still human – naked, climbing the stairs

where none of us has lived for years.
Who put the light on? Forty watts,

enough to see his thread arms reach up.
Look away. Count to ten. Hope he's gone.

But on he goes, a dogged mountaineer, hauling
himself up risers with carpet pile for rope.

My old room whispers – remember
angry footfall, you clinging to sheets?

I could improvise – a match-box bed –
or crush him with my thumb.

Instead, I coax him onto an Evening News
as you would a grounded moth but could I

pitch him from a window? I settle him
on the landing chair, on the edge

of a crevasse, a tear in the plush. He'll be safe,
harmless, free to roam in the fireproof foam.

DUSKING THROUGH WAVES   WENDY HOLBOROW

She swims
                dusking through waves

until sun & moon collide
feet trailing benthos
legs nudging sargassum
           & creatures of the shallow-deep
that scrut around in the rufus hours of evening:

spiny fish nibble toes,   scuttling crabs pinch.

A porpoise reclines on the purple headland
(head inclines towards her, snoutling, scenting)
dives into the sea with purpose,
a seal flumps along the rocks

as she flails arms in the turbulent sea.

                *

She sits on the beach,
                waves larruping her feet,
waves approaching / reproaching the shore –
struggling to find a hold on the slope of shingle.

A mongering of rumour from distant voices,
au(burn) hair s(moulders) in this rubified light,

she ruminates on her troubles & the dolour of her life,
enters her own subconscious
like edging into a dark, disturbing cave
until the polished air of a hopeless dawn rubs the sky.

*

She swims
                      dawning through waves

until moon & sun collude
drifting through benthos & seaweed
                & creatures of the shallow-deep
until the porpoise returns to the rock
until the seal has swum away
until tendrils of auburn are visible
haunting towards the hunted horizon.

*

She swims
                      drowning through waves

until life and death collide –
no longer does she tread the ocean floor
                nor nudge creatures from the shallow-deep.

Waves larrup her lungs
waves approach / reproach her
arms flail as she surrenders to the esurient sea

THE BEST OF BOTH WORLDS   ESTHER MURBACH

By now she has figured out how best to travel light. Commuting between the home where she was born and the new home where she feels reborn has become routine. She has her handbag dangling from her right shoulder to the left hip on a long strap and the backpack riding on her back. Both are smaller and lighter than even Ryanair allows. They practically pack themselves, her hands hardly needing directions from the brain any more.

Once airborne, in the Nowhereland between two worlds, her soul floats like an astronaut in space. For the duration of the flight she can't say where she's really grounded. In what she leaves behind? In what lies ahead, the joys of her choice? Not that her new world is perfect, far from it. But it holds more lightness. No old baggage there.

'Escapism!' a voice taunts at the back of her mind. She chooses to ignore it.

Landing in Dublin Airport usually also initiates a tentative touchdown of the soul. At first hopping like erstwhile Neil Armstrong on the moon in low gravity, the soul gets less agitated on the way to the westbound bus. Once inside, it settles down to a premonition of homecoming. As the bustle of the urban area gets left behind and the coach is passing endless pastures dotted with cows and sheep and horses, the soul finds soil again.

The coach finally turns into Galway Central Bus Station, the last lap of her journey lies ahead. She gets into the first of the taxis lined up in front of the terminal and tells the driver where to go. Home. To her chosen home, her apartment in Salthill.

Cold air hits her when she unlocks the door. Quickly she presses switches to activate the amenities of modern comfort – light, heating, hot water. She checks the fridge, gets the strongest plastic bag from her stock in the still cold hot press and hurries down to the shop next door. By the time she returns heavily laden, the first warm air from the radiators is battling the damp chill inside.

Outside it is still light, the dusk slowly descending, ornating the evening sky with a pink-rimmed cloud. The trees in front of her window shiver in wintry nakedness, their branches wiggling in the wind as if painting pictures on the horizon with delicate brushes.

    She settles down on the sofa under the cuddly blanket. Sandwich is cold but tea is hot. Feet are warming up, so is her soul. She's made it again to her haven. She slips into a state of meditation, eyes half-closed but still fixed on the scenery outside.

    Slowly the pink cloud dissolves. The trees transition from decorative sketches to skeletal tangles against the darkening canvas of nightfall.

A rap on the door startles her. Reluctantly, she peels the blanket from her body, shuffles to the door. In the dimly lit hall outside a familiar form glares at her. It's her heavy heart from the old home. Once again, it can't help following her.

STICKLEBACK   IAIN TWIDDY

Autumn, when the river oaks were thinning
into the fence wires and bare tugging of grass,
and the surface would dull with stuns of wind,
there was still a chance, although the water

gulped at the rubber like a stone-cold bath,
still a chance of a nervy, patched straggler,
a tiddler finning a see-through stretch;
still a glimpse of slipping the net behind,

held-breathily, into the scoosh and scull
– like a wand-swish – into the lift and flash
flipping its silver in the blub of silt.
Stroked, it triggered, tigered with olive-blush

and spearhead grey, the shock-eye like the sky
below ground, like rock split into opal.
Pinching his neck, we inspected the spikes:
felt him pulse, how he might burst like a pea-pod.

What were they there for? Were they poisonous,
like the Amazon frog in the annual?
Would they draw blood, fresh as the bulging haws,
pin like a spindle for a hundred years?

We put him in the bucket for a bit,
let him turn and glum in the muck-frayings,
till it got tanking cold, till it was clear
there'd be no others; then just put him back,

watched him zip off through the leafy water,
smooth as the scent of a rose from its thorns,
into distance, a prick of feeling
I can't put my finger on, even still.

MARIE-THÉRÈSE WALTER MOURNS THE DEATH OF HER FORMER LOVER PABLO PICASSO   ADAM TAVEL

ago when I was beautiful the sun
would kiss the leathered muscles of my walk
till Paris bent its smirking genius down
to flash his practised appetite and woo
my breasts my head unreal which lured the world
each time his canvas froze me snaking lithe
on sofas chairs a ghost invisible
was making love to me against my will
the vines outsized these symbols obvious
and strangling tame my belly's swollen rune
his wife the moon across the boulevard
but now forever night balloons his fame
O daughter made from yellow lust we hang
in frames so patrons clutch their coats and gasp

TO CHOOSE MICHAEL G. SMITH

after a poem by W.S. Merwin

I am held by the voice
and after turning more pages
cranes arrive
from a distant horizon
to follow a boy
and I find myself
walking a dusty trail
along the Rio Grande
in light still dripping with dew
the migrating sandhills circling
calling to one another
in their singular voice
and called
I walk not missing
my name everything not
needing a question tied to
its answer
my voice feeling
right because I woke
and chose to listen

SEEING THE LIGHT   DEIRDRE NALLY

*E*ve has started buying tins of marrowfat peas and Campbell's tomato soup, hiding them behind the canned lentils and organic dried apricots, where the architect will not see them. She is certain now that, in a bright fitted kitchen somewhere, Peter is concealing jars of olives and preserved lemons – placing them, perhaps, behind the boxes of breakfast cereal where the nurse from the Mater will never find them, will never know that she and Peter continue to dance together in illicit harmony.

All that spring and summer they had been looking at houses. The kind of houses she likes with stained glass windows, mosaic tiles, and the stale overlay of other lives. The kind of houses he likes, with brand new open-plan rooms and well-lit corners.

They had debated in shiny ensuites, argued on creaking staircases, quarrelled in furnished showhouses and fallen out in tangled gardens. On a tarmacadamed drive in Kildare she had finally flung the ring at him, and walked alone to the bus stop, waiting for Peter to call her back across the sudden silence.

She is in a pub off Capel Street when she hears that Peter is engaged to the nurse from the Mater. It is Christmas week and she has squeezed up to the bar to get a round in for her colleagues. Across the crush of people she sees an acquaintance from the old days, pushing towards her to say hello.

'Did you hear,' he asks, 'about Peter? He's got engaged, to a nurse from the Mater.'

'Oh yes, I think I heard something about it,' she lies. She leaves her order on the bar and shoves her way to the door and out onto the street and walks all the way home. Walking and walking through the cold December night while all around her everyone continues to celebrate as if it's just another ordinary Christmas.

*

On the morning of her wedding, she is in her childhood bedroom pinning on her veil with white hairclips when her mother comes in and sits on the bed.

'You know,' she says, 'there's no shame in changing your mind. And I will support you whatever you decide to do.'

She decides she will marry the architect, and drifts down the aisle in the white satin dress that makes her look like a beautiful marble statue. As he places the ring on her finger she hears, across a distance, the rattle of gold on tarmacadam.

She and the architect had bought the third house they saw. An Edwardian semi in need of much work, but with a sea view if you hang out of the spare room at the right angle. They sand and polish and paint. They find the right fireplace in a salvage yard in Inchicore and drive to Belfast to bid on door handles and brass light fixtures. They preserve the timber floors and dismantle the unsightly porch. When it is finished they relax on the lawn and open the bottle of Perrier Jouet the architect has been saving for the right occasion.

'Sure we won't know the difference,' Peter had said, coming out of Tesco with a bottle of Prosecco the day they got engaged. He had filled wine glasses to brimming and they had toasted to their future, leaning against the garden wall in the early evening warmth.

'To the future,' said the architect, holding the stem in his long elegant fingers.

'To the future,' she says, raising her glass and watching the sun dip and sink behind the gabled roof.

*

When Flora is born they are in agreement about her name. The architect does not argue for something less pretentious, like Aoife or Aisling. Eve does not protest that everyone calls their kids those names. The architect does not say that Flora sounds like something you spread on your toast. She does not throw the baby name book at him so that he can pick it up and laugh and they can start all over again.

Flora slips easily into her name, a flowerlike child who likes to plant seeds with her mother, pressing them into the soil with long graceful fingers.

'Don't push them in too deep,' Eve warns her.

'Why not?' Flora likes to bury down as far as she can, to where there might be worms wriggling in the damp earth.

Eve points at the sky. 'They need to be near the light, so it can keep them strong and allow them to grow.'

She buys oven chips and Donegal Catch, pushing them into the third drawer of the freezer, beside the sliced brown bread with pumpkin seeds.

*

The old convent grounds opposite them have been sold off for a small development of houses. The architect makes representations on behalf of the residents' association and drafts an objection for the planning department.

'It will be good for Flora,' says Eve's mother, who does not care about unsympathetic brickwork and the felling of ancient oak trees. 'It will bring young families into the area. She'll have some friends of her own age.'

The architect organises a lobby group, and writes enraged letters to *The Irish Times*. The builders are ordered to alter the window design and build twenty-five houses instead of the planned forty. The diggers arrive and the architect fumes.

The following summer Eve and her mother take a nosy look around the showhouse. 'Very nice,' says her mother, 'but you have to bring the bins through the hall. That's always a mistake. Young couples don't think of that.'

Eve wanders through the open-plan rooms, breathing in the smell of new carpet and paint. Her mother goes upstairs to admire the ensuite and Eve pushes through the viewers in the narrow hall and out the front door.

She buys a bottle of HP sauce and leaves it right in the middle of the shelf, beside the sherry vinegar. If the architect asks, she will say it adds depth to her boeuf bourguignon.

Flora's seeds grow and bloom, but she is no longer interested. She squirms as Eve brushes her hair and pleads to be let down from the table so that she can run to the other side of the road where there are trampolines and Barbie bikes and she can join the little girls who sit in circles on sandstone driveways, serving their dolls tea out of pink plastic cups.

The house is quiet and suddenly still without her. Eve moves restlessly through its shadows.

She has begun to take risks. She buys Peter's aftershave and places it on the shelf above the bed, barely out of sight behind the photoframes and candle holders. And somewhere, she knows, the oak and ember scent of the perfume she has worn for twenty years is sitting in a mirrored bathroom cabinet, mingling dangerously with The Nurse from the Mater's duty free Eternity.

It is almost time for Flora to come back for lunch. She goes downstairs and waits.

*

The architect needs some Forms of Tender dropped in to an office on the other side of town. She has nothing better to do. Walking back to the bus stop she calls in to the post office beside the big supermarket on the main road. The car park is busy and a middle-aged couple load groceries into the back of a grey estate. The husband straightens up and calls something to the two sturdy boys who wait beside the car. He spots Eve and smiles widely.

It is Peter.

He is pleased to see her. He really is. He introduces her to his wife, whose name is not The Nurse from the Mater, but Elaine; and to the two strapping boys, Eoin and Cormac.

'They eat us out of house and home,' he says, waving towards the boot at the bulging bags that hold no secrets or regrets.

'Would you look who's talking,' Elaine says cheerfully. There is no doubt that Peter has put on weight. His face is jowly, his t-shirt stretched across his stomach. Elaine is small and neat and mildly curious to meet Eve.

'I've heard about you. Only good things, of course,' she laughs, and Peter laughs and so Eve laughs too.

No, she says, she does not live around here, she is just passing through.

The sturdy boys are bored and scuff their trainers against the wheels of the grey estate.

'Well, it's been lovely to meet you,' says Elaine.

'You're looking great, you really are,' says Peter.

They climb into the car and drive away, Peter, Elaine, Eoin and Cormac, and Eve walks on up the hill to the bus stop.

Later that night she goes through the cupboards and shelves with a black plastic bag. Burrowing into the damp recesses of the wheelie bin she wedges the bag into a corner, pushing it down as far as it will go, down where the light of day cannot reach it.

WALKING WITHOUT SNOWSHOES   JOHN D. KELLY

I light a beeswax candle, each day
on the inside sill of a front window
and go out again searching, walking

without snowshoes; struggling alone
through blanket lies of convincing snow
in cold-grey dawns of regretting, sinking.

They say that hope of finding you alive
is fast-fading as my own footprints fade
but still I walk for miles . . . and miles

imagining your faint breathing –
between words – in gentle songlines
whispering through my dreams.

Are they too to become just an echo –
yet another loss for me (a circling ass)
in this desert? I always seem to find

the last straw to break my own back;
never believing myself worthy enough
to hold the weight of such sacredness –

such pure lightness . . . lightly. I can't
bear to contemplate that you might be
like a grounded angel – white on white

under white; further hidden in the dead-
centred middle of a field; re-covered
in other fresh lies – heavy drifts

so deep that I only sink in deeper
as I try to reach you; and then . . .
as I tread on frozen water, cold crystals

seem to turn into white-hot sand, as
paradigms shift. I pray now for a caravan
of camels – that I might reach you.

COCHIN HENS   ANTHONY LAWRENCE

I can hear the cochin hens raking for worms
under the wormwood: a comforting sound
like a stove ticking in a slide-show of light.

They move carefully, as though sorting
through material at a rummage sale
on raised beds like straw-covered tables.

Each morning my daughter would call
and they'd run, trailing blue leggings
for the grain she'd scatter on the lawn.

I can see her enter the chicken shed
turning at the door to close her umbrella
then draw it in the way squid conform

to their ink-dark folds before vanishing.
And when she looks up as if checking
for rain, the scar on her neck gleams

like a weld-seam: a raised, upper-case
Z from surgery after a scalding.
The day she was born, her arrival fast

and sure as being surprised is counter-
point to premature, the fibres of her
nerves had been disengaged. Extremes

of temperature or a fall, while running
were potentially fatal. Unsupervised
she would have swallowed soup or oats

straight off the boil. Now, in her absence
I can hear her mimicry of the tiny
expectant sounds the hens made

when, having found something worthy
of scrutiny, they would gather in quiet
concentration, as we did, to watch them eat.

A DOG'S LIFE　　　　　　　　　　MERCEDES LAWRY

The happiness of dogs slides into
      the moon's shadow and such
      a quiet collision, sea oats rustling
      the last prayer

of a hopeful child dissolving in summer's
      thick air.

What else did the soothsayer say?
The lucky are gathered at the shore
sharing their false gods,
      a soft moment, a caress.

If anyone chooses to leave, now
      is the time.

Dogs may love you. Dogs may become
      mirrors, eventually,
      tarnished.

When all is said and done, there will be
      a few crumbs, soiled napkins,
      skewed memories and the same

smiling dogs we began with, washed in the light
      of the sun, hungry
      but strangely patient.

I, OBJECT — EMILY WOODWORTH

Crowbar: an implement used to pry things open, pull out nails, or bash in windows.
Johnny: a guy with a crowbar.
Jane: a gal with a vendetta.

The Window: once transparent and fragile, now shattered, its remains christening the floor of the farmhouse in mixed shards like knives and glitter.

'I'll go first,' says Jane to Johnny as she pushes the Crowbar aside.

'Typical,' says the Crowbar to itself. 'I do all the work, they get all the glory.'

'Quiet,' says Johnny.

Glass pieces fringe the window frame like the remaining teeth of a veteran boxer. Jane removes her dark sweatshirt and covers the surviving glass. She unlocks the knob of the door and swings it open rapidly. It creaks once, then stops with a nervous tremor.

The three look down at the glass ruins beyond and Jane tiptoes ahead, crunching unseen grist beneath her Converse.

'You should have let me attack the doorjamb,' says the Crowbar, its voice like the clangour of an aluminium baseball bat hitting a homer.

Johnny hushes the Crowbar again.

'I should be used with finesse,' says the Crowbar, quieter. 'You could have bashed that window in with anything – a hammer, a rock, your fist. Why bring me anyway?'

'For the job, dumbass,' Jane hisses over her shoulder. She stands on clean pine boards now, removing her shoes. Johnny picks his way through the glass more loudly.

'Don't step that way, Johnny,' says the Crowbar, 'to the right – what job?'

'Would you shut up?' Jane says, almost breaking her whisper as she sets her shoes aside gently, belly up. Johnny makes it through the window spatter and scraps his shoes too.

Jane signals their next move with a wave of her false nails. They make their way through the kitchen, a 1970s drop ceiling event with yellow glass windows and a dinosaur refrigerator that roars to life as they pass.

Clementine: an orange tabby cat of the mouse–hunting profession; consummate business person, unwilling to interfere in others' affairs.

'Don't give us any trouble, pussy,' says Johnny, brandishing the Crowbar.

'Stop swinging me like that!' says the Crowbar.

'I'll just be leaving,' remarks the orange tabby coolly as she trots with noiseless padded paws to a pet door.

'A pet door! You could have just unlocked that door from outside and saved me a night's work,' says the Crowbar in a huff, a nervous pinging in its metallic voice, like a dime dropping in a copper bucket. 'By the way, I think this is far enough. Why not leave me in the kitchen while you steal whatever it is you're after?' Johnny walks on. 'I feel a bit queasy, really. Best to stop off and catch my breath. It's all that almost–swinging you did at the cat, I'll warrant –'

'Can't you shut that thing up?' says Jane with a venomous look at Johnny. The whites of her brown eyes are lit ghostly from the porch bulb outside, streaming through the broken window.

Johnny tightens his grip on the Crowbar and seethes, 'Not another word, you.' Then they continue creeping down the hall. As they go, Jane begins trembling.

'Hey, you cool?' asks Johnny from behind.

'No, that's what I've been saying!' says the Crowbar.

'Give me that thing,' Jane says, ignoring them both and taking a deep breath. She has stopped outside a door on the left side of the hallway. It is open just enough for a cat to slither in and out, an arrangement made by Clementine against the better judgement of her roommate. Jane knows what is beyond the door. She has spent hours at a time there while her price was negotiated. She gently puts her hand on the glossy wood, but does not push yet.

Doris: roommate to Clementine; a farm woman to the core; a Madame during droughts; a rough character pretending to sleep, having woken at the crackle of glass a minute earlier.

Shotgun: an implement used to hurl tiny objects at a velocity high enough to kill; only deadly when loaded; current condition: unloaded.

Bedroom Door: a paranoid criminal's last alarm clock.

Doris hears the signal of the door, but not the footfalls that bring Jane closer to her bedside. Her Shotgun attempts to whisper something to her. Her hand tightens on the Shotgun, stifling its warning. The pillow absorbs her sweat. She is facing away from Jane.

Jane can see the outline of Doris' ample hip beneath the light blue quilt. Johnny begins to follow, but she signals with a flick of her hand that he should stay his progress. She creeps closer. The Crowbar tries to speak, but finds itself hampered by Jane's steel grip. She draws up to the side of the bed.

Doris has heard the creak of the door and what she believes to be Jane's halting footsteps at the threshold, but she has mistaken the footfalls of clumsy Johnny for her cash cow. She wonders why Jane has stopped, and for a moment her heart swells with gladness as she thinks that Jane must still love her after all.

As Doris imagines Jane's slender figure and silky hair, Jane lifts the Crowbar, her aim fixed on Doris' head.

But as she swings back her grip loosens and the Crowbar screams a metallic shriek of agony, like a dull table–saw defeated by plywood. 'Don't make me!' it says, and Doris whips around and out of bed in one move, the Shotgun trained on Jane.

Johnny flicks on the light.

Doris' bed is twin–sized. Jane knows she could reach Doris' skull across it. But Jane also knows that the Shotgun is empty. The shells are in her very own pocket. The Shotgun tries to speak.

'Shut up, you,' snaps Doris, her voice made gravel by pipe smoking and dust. 'So, you come to kill the woman that raised you?'

'Yes,' says Jane.

'Seems like you forgot a few details,' says Doris.

'I guess it seems that way,' says Jane.

'Where have you been these days, anyways?' asks Doris.

'Thinking.'

'Don't go making jokes, I was asking a serious question.'

'You can't talk to her like that,' says Johnny from the door.

'This ain't your affair, Johnny. On top of being almost kin, Jane and I have a business arrangement and she's the one as broke the contract,' says Doris, 'making me the wronged party here.' Then to Jane she adds, 'You know I ain't gonna represent you to the best clients anymore after this.'

'Surely, we can come to some peaceable arrangement,' says the Crowbar meekly.

'I never wanted your representation,' Jane says.

'What's all this, now? What happened to "thank you, mama Doris"? Without me you'd have starved eight or nine times since your folks passed. Your uncle was a smart man having me look out for you.'

'Yeah, well my uncle is not my guardian anymore. Had a wee accident in Omaha this morning. Seems to me that ends any arrangement there was between us two,' says Jane.

Doris slides her bottom lip into the gap where her top right canine used to reside, something she always does when she is turning things around in her mind.

'Alright, then, pay your debt and we're done,' she says.

'I don't owe you anything,' says Jane. These words cut Doris like shards of glass from a broken window.

'I invested food and clothes and shelter and time and … and love into you. I intend on being repaid,' she says, knowing she's letting too much emotion show through. She grips the Shotgun even tighter to steady herself. 'Now, I've got the gun here, not you. Either you fulfil your contract the way I want and live the rest of your life – what I would prefer – or I can shoot you and get compensation out of whatever organs don't have buckshot in them.'

'Oh, I think the first option sounds jolly,' says the Crowbar in a panic.

'Shut up,' says Johnny from the door.

'There's just one problem with your plan, Doris,' says Jane.

'What's that?'

'Your Shotgun. It's been trying to tell you something since this conversation started, and I think you ought to listen,' says Jane.

But Doris doesn't have to listen. Her eyes widen like a jack rabbit on speed. She knows.

Crowbar: an implement used to pry things open, pull out nails, or bash in windows, skulls.

'Oh, how could you?' cries the Crowbar. 'How could you make me? I told you I was just coming along to bash in the window, and now this! Oh, mercy, there are brains on me – organic matter! This isn't what I was designed for, this isn't manual labour, this isn't what I mean when I think of "demolition". Oh, I shall be tainted in the eyes of my brethren. Ah, me! Ah, me! Ah, me!'

As the Crowbar melts into chaotic whimpers of self–loathing, Jane sits beside the object that once was Doris, arranging the corpse–woman's chin–length grey hair around the split in her skull, as if dressing a doll.

Johnny has averted his eyes, and does not look up. 'Is it done?'

Jane smiles and sighs and stands up with the Crowbar.

'Alright, let's get you washed up,' she says. She pushes past Johnny and into the kitchen, where she scrubs the mewling murderer clean.

Clementine enters the house again. She raises an eyebrow, then shrugs.

'She should have listened to the gun,' she says, then flicks her tail disdainfully and stalks off into the night again.

Jane and Johnny sit down to replace their shoes. Jane's socks have blood on the toes, but she doesn't notice. As they tie their laces in silence, the Crowbar jabbers.

'I'll have to stand trial for this, I say. I'll tell the jury I had no choice, but will they believe me? No. I warrant there will be not even one appliance of destruction on the jury – not a wrecking ball, or pliers, or bolt cutters. No, I'll get stuck with construction contraptions:

drills, screwdrivers, nails. Sure I'll have an "impartial" hammer as a judge. But we all know hammers tend more towards construction. It won't be a sledgehammer on the bench, I can tell you that right now. What happened to trial by peers? No constructor could ever understand what it is to be a destructor. How could they – always building things up, always making the world more orderly. And what am I to them but a lowly – '

'That's enough,' says Jane, hefting the Crowbar in her right hand as she and Johnny exit through the side door to avoid the broken glass. They walk to Johnny's car and set out for Texas. From there Mexico. Jane throws the Crowbar in the back of the rusty blue pickup and gets in the passenger seat. The Crowbar lands with a thud beside Johnny's toolbox and is taken into custody immediately, his fate to be decided at dawn. Johnny starts the car and they drive off. Jane sets her hand on his thigh.

Ruskin: a rat with the scent of blood in his nose and an empty belly; happy to pay full price and tip well for any well-prepared meal; currently testing a dish called Doris.

Daybreak: the moment Jane knows she can no longer be bought and sold like a tool; the moment the Crowbar is flung from the truck onto the side of the road, sentence: death by rust; the moment Clementine first tries a new rat recipe; the moment Johnny knows he is a fugitive; the moment this story ends.

A NIGHT AT THE THEATRE   SEAN KELLY

You stepped out of your shoes in the hallway,
walked upstairs while I closed the front door –
heartburn you said.

The kitchen clock ticks louder without you.
A last drink with a fruit bowl for company.
The wine has been open for days.
Steaks defrost by the sink.
Knives wait patiently in the block.

You must be asleep by now.
I hear you cough.
My lies hang like cheap shirts
behind the wardrobe door.
For no reason that I can name,
you have not walked away.

I go to the window.
The moon is thin, barely alive.
Across town,
bus stops are deserted,
the theatre locked.

Rosalind, now blind, sits on an empty stage.

NOT TO GO BACK — VANESSA KIRKPATRICK

Not to go back
not to ask
why you have found love
buried deep
only in the most difficult places

but to know
you held it in your hands,
you knew the warm
expansive feel of it

Not to go back
not to ask
why you stand bone-weary,
lethargy threatening
to pin your mind
back to its darkest corners

but to keep walking,
to somehow summon
lightness again
to your step

Not to go back
not to ask
how you came alone to this beach
where the future approaches
too quickly
in dark mouths of waves

only to watch
seabirds on the foaming crests
rise and take flight
on currents of air

only to hope
in words
you might find wings

DON JUAN IN 30 LINES — CRAIG KURTZ

Two hundred years[1], it's come to this –
we want our verse exiguous;
now *Don Juan*, that epic book,
must be one page, a minute's look.
He was a blithe lad, led astray
by vixen lust, then chased away
where, shipwrecked, he attained true love –
minutia we got rid of;
that romance blocked, again to sea
where Turks brought him to slavery;
then cross-dressed in a seraglio,
Juan had exploits we forgo;
prolix Byron, let's give 'im props
but, these days, 30 lines is tops.
There was a war Juan joined in
and rescued a Muslim urchin;
this saga once had folks engrossed,
but brevity's now uppermost;
then on to Catherine the Great's
court, where the plot expatiates;
Juan her lover, Byron wrote
two cantos, now lopped to a mote –
'cause, nowadays, attention's gone
a minute on, per *au courant*.
From there, our hero England went
to laud freedom and parliament;
while getting robbed, his mugger shot –
but that is all the time we got.
Today, most reading's cursory,
so fare thee well, old epopee.

[1] Byron began the 16,000 line, unfinished, 'comic epic' in September 1818.

THE DARE   TANYA FARRELLY

Gary was the one who'd spotted the number. They'd spilled from the train, crossed over the footbridge and descended to the platform; an ungainly gaggle of fifth years, exuberant that they'd made it to the mid-term break. It was on one of those sticky notes, illuminous pink, and in a spidery black hand it read Debra.

Gary stooped and picked up the paper. 'Hey Julian, have you lost your girlfriend's number?'

Julian leaned in to examine the note, then swiped it from his fingers. 'Whihoo. A number at last!' he said, holding the pink paper aloft as he pirouetted down the platform. The rest of the lads laughed and he stopped prancing to pass it round. 'Like in the song,' Danny said. 'What?' 'You know… her name was Debra …' he sang, but he didn't get a chance to continue as a hand was clamped over his mouth.

'Somebody should ring it,' Julian said. 'Gary – you're the one that found it.'

Gary shook his head. 'Go on, triple dare you,' the shout went up. Gary looked at the note. Debra – nice name. Not spelt in the usual way either. Maybe she was one of those Italian girls studying at the language school on the seafront – dark wavy hair, and tanned legs showing under cropped jeans.

'Okay, okay,' he said. He took out his phone, tapped in the number. The lads hung around outside the station waiting while the phone buzzed in Gary's left ear. 'Yeeaaaaaah?' The voice was muffled, sounded like the speaker had been woken. 'Hello, is that Debra?' Gary said, not having a clue what he was going to say next. There was a silence, then some unintelligible sound, yawning maybe. 'Who the hell wants to know?' she said. Gary hung up. Whoever Debra was, she didn't sound like she'd appreciate a crank call.

'What? What happened?' one of the lads asked.

'Nothing.'

'What do you mean nothing? What did she say?'

'It wasn't her.' Gary stuck the post-it note in his pocket.

'What do you mean it wasn't her?' Julian asked.

'I don't know. Maybe it was a wrong number.'

Gary was in his room doing homework when his phone rang. 'Who's this?' the voice asked. 'Julian,' he said. He recognised Debra's voice. 'Why did you call me before?' Gary looked at his maths copybook and deciding it would be less complicated, he told the truth. 'It was a dare. We found your number on a sticky note.' 'Where?' the woman asked. 'Bray station.' She breathed heavily into the phone. He wondered if she might be drunk. 'Bray,' she repeated. 'Yeah, Bray.' In the background, Gary could hear a strange noise. It sounded like a dog whining, or maybe it was a television. 'Look, I'm sorry,' he said. 'It was a dumb joke.' The woman didn't answer. After a moment, she spoke again. 'I'm going to kill myself, Julian,' she said. 'You're the last person I'll ever speak to. Isn't that strange? We've never even met.'

Gary had been doodling on his copybook. Now, he threw down the pen. This was no fifteen-year-old exchange student. This was a woman who needed help. 'Don't do that,' he said. 'Why not?' the woman asked. 'Well, what about your family, your friends?' 'I don't have any friends,' she said. 'Where are you?' Gary asked, picking up the pen again. 'I'll come see you.' 'What? Are you going to be my friend, Julian?' the woman laughed. But it wasn't really a laugh – more a forced cackle. 'If you want,' he said. 'I'd … I'd like to meet you.' 'Why? Why would you want to meet me?' Gary looked round, trying to think of something to say. 'Because you sound interesting,' he said. 'Mad you mean. Suicidal.' She laughed again. 'Why did you say you called me?' She was definitely drunk. 'For your address,' he said. 'I'm coming to help you.'

Gary stood outside the grey terraced house and put his finger on the bell. The sharp buzz that he expected didn't sound so he couldn't tell if it was working. Instead, he raised the brass knocker and listened to it echo through the eerily quiet house. In the porch, several pot plants wilted; leaves shrivelled by the sun. A no junk mail sign on the letterbox was ignored, it's gaping mouth stuffed with fliers. He jumped when he felt something at his legs. When he looked down a small grey cat miaowed up at him. Gary wasn't fond of cats. Not since his grandmother's ginger Tom had sunk its teeth into his arm, and so he eyed this cat sceptically as it butted its small head against him.

Thinking about his grandmother gave Gary an idea. He shooed the cat away and lifted the first pot plant. There was nothing beneath but a brown streak on the lino where a long time ago, water had run. He turned over each pot until finally the one closest the wall yielded what he'd been hoping to find, a single brass key like the one for his own front door.

Gary stepped into the hall. The house was dark. On the bannister a blue raincoat hung, and a pair of mud-caked boots poked from under the stairs. Upstairs, he heard voices. When he stopped by the banisters to listen, he discovered it was a radio talking. 'Hello?' he called. Nobody answered. Cautiously, he climbed the first few steps of the stairs. He almost let out a yelp when something brushed past him and he realised that the cat must have darted in ahead of him when he'd opened the door. 'Hello?' he said again, this time raising his voice. The last thing he wanted to do was to frighten the woman.

Just as he reached the landing there was a thump. 'Debra?' Gary called. The woman's name sounded strange on his lips. There was a groan, followed by the cat's miaowing. 'How did you get in here, huh?' he heard the woman say, but she was talking to the cat who'd jumped onto the bed where she was perched. Gary tapped on the door frame and she looked up, startled. 'What the fuck are you doing in here?' she said, grabbing the bottle from the bedside locker. Gary lifted his hands to protect himself as she flung the bottle, barely missing his head. It crashed against the wall, but didn't smash and rolled along the carpet. 'I'm Julian,' Gary said, as the woman got to her feet and stood there swaying. 'We talked on the phone, remember?'

'Julian, Christ you're a child,' she said, and he suddenly felt very self-conscious standing there in his school uniform. The woman sat on the edge of the bed again. She was wearing nothing but a t-shirt and she didn't bother to cover her bare legs.

'You said you were going to kill yourself,' Gary said.

She took a packet of cigarettes from the locker, put one between her lips and groped round for a lighter. 'Yeah, well, decided I couldn't be bothered,' she said. 'You got a light, Julian?' He shook his head. 'Actually, my name's Gary.' The woman laughed. 'I prefer Julian,' she said. The cigarette bobbed between her lips, unlit.

Gary looked round the darkened room. It was a mess. A mountain of clothes piled on a chair had erupted onto the floor and lay strewn across the carpet. He stepped round them and with a swift movement, pulled back the curtains. Debra put a hand to her eyes. 'Jesus, Julian,' she said. He stood by the window, waited until she lowered her hand from her eyes. She looked round, dazed, the cigarette growing soggy in her mouth.

'When did you last eat?' Gary asked. Debra shrugged, kicked at another empty bottle by the bed. 'The doctor says fluids are what's important.' 'Have you seen a doctor?' She laughed. 'Doctors know shit about my problem.' Debra leaned on her hands and pushed herself back against the pillows. She drew her legs up, the t-shirt too short to cover her. Gary looked away. He thought of his mother, how her legs had become bird-like, too thin almost to support her. Debra, in the harsh light, looked about his mother's age. She'd have been fifty on her next birthday. Thinking of her made his eyes sting, and he turned abruptly from the woman.

'I'll make you something to eat,' he said. Debra rubbed the cat's belly as it lay on its back and stretched its paws towards her. The kitchen was surprisingly clean, everything in its place. Unfortunately, all he found in the fridge was an outdated carton of eggs and some sour milk. He closed it again and looked in the cupboards. This time he found a tin of porridge and a carton of condensed milk, which he figured would be better than nothing.

'Jeez, Julian, you're well-trained,' the woman said. She'd found a lighter some place and now smoke wafted round the room, curling upwards. Gary watched her poke the porridge with the spoon, the cigarette still in her mouth. 'Why did you want to kill yourself?' he asked. Debra pushed the porridge round, but didn't eat. 'Because it's all gone,' she said. 'Everything. Everyone.' She sounded, suddenly, sober.

'What do you mean?' Gary asked. 'Where did they go?'

'What? Nowhere,' she said. 'They were never here to begin with.' She waved her cigarette, the bowl slid to the edge of the tray, stopped just short of falling. Gary was beginning to wish he'd never made that call, had never come here to help this strange woman.

'My mother died,' he said. 'She didn't want to. She fought till there was no fight left in her.' Those were his dad's words when he'd tried to console Gary.

Debra took a puff on the cigarette. 'She's lucky,' she said. 'Why would anyone want to hang round this dump?'

Gary felt the anger deep in his stomach. He wanted to take the bowl and smash it, like the woman had, against the wall. Watch the porridge drip down the pink paintwork. What right had she to want to take her own life? 'You don't know what you're talking about,' he said. 'Look at you sprawled here feeling sorry for yourself.'

The woman gave him a look. 'Don't judge me, Julian,' she said.

'It's Gary,' he said.

'Whatever. If you came here looking for another mother, boy did you get the wrong number ...'

'I came here to help,' Gary said, angry with himself for the catch in his voice. This woman could never compare to his mother, but he'd thought maybe he could help, maybe he could save her.

'You should go on your way now, Julian,' the woman said. 'If I see your mother, I'll tell her hello.' She puffed on the cigarette, picked up the empty bottle from the floor and stared at it hard. She continued looking at it until Gary turned and stomped out of the room.

In anger, Gary pulled the bunch of fliers from the mouth of the letterbox, letting it snap shut. Among them there were letters, half a dozen of them, unopened, bearing the government stamp. He lifted one from the pile. Ms Debra O'Connor, it said. URGENT! Gary glanced up the stairs. There were voices coming from the woman's room again. She'd turned the radio up loud. Another bunch of letters lay scattered on the hall table. Curious, he lifted one that had been torn open. The address in the corner read Social Services. He glanced down at the content below. Three short sentences informed Debra that her appeal for custody of her daughter Lara had been turned down by the High Court. Gary stood there, paper in hand, wondering if he should go back up there, give the woman her mail. The voices on the radio grew louder. Gary stacked the letters in a pile on the table and let himself out the door.

CROW
V.P. LOGGINS

Having seen him many times
On the side of the road where
His black feathers glisten as
His beak dips into one morsel
Or another – a dead rabbit, cat,
Squirrel, some unrecognisable
And bloody thing – it comes
As a surprise when I hear

The commotion of crows above
The spring holly and go to inspect
The cause of this cacophony
And find the speckle-breasted,
Long-tailed hawk balanced,
Green and shadowed, on a branch
Where it stands atop a crow
Tearing feathers away and snapping

Flesh out of the dead bird's chest.
Dipping its head it looks about,
Cautious, careful, committed, concerned,
Concentrating on the task of beaking
Into and through the carrion – the crow –
Who must have swallowed terror's ice
When, predator turning prey, it saw
An eye reflected in another's talons.

THE STONE MASONS' YARD REVISITED
EAMONN LYNSKEY

(after Canaletto)

Because I cannot pass where work is doing
these stone masons busy at their craft
detain me, bell tower rising up behind them,
canal waters flowing silkily past.

I'd half-expected they'd have given way
to office-block and supermarket landscape,
but they labour still as first I saw them,
hammers poised to chip and split and shape.

Here's one who leans into his task, his eye
fixed on the point will take the chisel's edge.
Another decorates a pediment,
another finishes off a polished ledge.

And so much happening else outside their yard –
small cameos of ordinary lives:
a cockerel struts along a window sill,
a woman turns to help a fallen child,

while others set their lines of wash to dance
so whitely, merrily in the morning breeze –
their men will home this evening, tired and dusty,
must have shirts tomorrow fresh and clean.

No devil's workshops here, no idle hands
in this tableau of life and daily living:
his a world of stern allotted duties
where all become what they are making, doing.

SNAPDRAGON   OLIVIA KENNY MCCARTHY

A late bee hovers
over the antirrhinum.
His wing beats angle him
to the puff of her
lemon lip.

I see him land, stumble
his weight on her.
She sucks him in.
Snap. Dragon.
The way she opens
and closes over him.

PERFECTION

Eager to calculate my points I skid over to Mama and ask to borrow the pen she keeps in her purse. Back in my seat I start reading the questions, hurriedly wanting to check off the ones that talk about me and add up my points.

Not yet, no, not yet. My eyes are quickly scanning and finding nothing. Aha! 'Moving Family Homes'. That's a whopping 300 points! But then I read the words in parenthesis: (within the last three years). Darn. We moved six years ago, and I can't really remember Ohio at all. I wonder if I could give myself 100 points.

'Arrival of A Younger Sibling'. I miss that one by a few years, too.

I finally get a few points toward the bottom for 'Returning from A Vacation' and 'Finishing the School Year and Moving Up A Grade.' A measly 30 points. I wanted to do a lot more adding. Some of them give 500 points. 'Divorce of Parents'.

I look over at Mama sitting on the ground of the doctor's waiting room, playing with Eduardo. He is pushing a wooden ball up and around circling wire. Then my mother follows with a green ball, chasing Eduardo around the 3D maze.

'Mama?'

'Yes, Bala?'

I run to her and show her the magazine. 'Mama, I hardly got any points.'

'What is it?' She looks over as she puts her arm around Eduardo, to make sure he doesn't wander off while she's not looking.

'This. You get points for the things that happen in your life.'

'Honey, this is for stress. It's good if you don't have a lot of points.'

'Do you think I can get points for moving from Ohio to McAllen? I know it was six years ago and the magazine says three, but can I still count it?'

'Bala, it's for parents worried about their kids. You don't have to take this. It's for kids who have trouble at home or at school.'

'Like if kids don't get on the Honor Roll?'

'Mhm, or maybe their father dies. Or their parents get a divorce.' I try to think of someone I can tell to take the test, but no one comes to mind. Everyone at school is fine. I think about the kids in books and movies wearing torn jeans or caps on backward. Do those kids really exist anywhere? If they do, are their parents taking this test?

'Eduardo Cepeda!'

In the doctor's office, after my brother's turn, I sit on the plastic paper and stare at my knees, wondering how they know to send my legs forward when Dr Gomez taps them with the rubber triangle. What would happen if my leg didn't move? What would it mean? I decide to not let my left leg fly and will it to stay still with my tensed jaw.

I stare. Out it flies. Rats.

We have a snack after we pick up Iko and arrive home. Opening three napkins, Mama places apple pieces, two cookies, and raisins and peanuts in three of the four squares. I pour myself a glass of orange juice and place it in my fourth square.

We go outside, bike our standard ten laps around the neighbourhood, and then get to play a game of basketball. I shower, read, kiss my father mandatorily when he arrives home and set the table for dinner. A few hours later, 'Goodnight, Bala. I love you,' and the door fits into its frame.

I am alone in my room with Pink Bear, God, and dark blue curtains letting in ripples from the universe as the wind breathes. It's the rarest of days, when we can have open windows, the cold front of sixty degrees letting us turn off the air conditioner for the night.

My lack of points from the magazine fizzles up my legs, through my stomach and up into my chest. 'Everything is too simple," the tingle mocks, the tiniest of nags, asking me about how and why I am living.

I hush it, the devil, the unclean. I kick down the comforter and kneel at the bottom of the bed, close my eyes, and prepare to open them and register the first star I see. If I make a wish upon the wrong star, my wish won't be granted, or worse, the opposite might occur.

Go!

Open and the star to the right is the brightest and I utter my wish and prayer, all desires and dreams wrapped up in God. 'Please help me be with you in heaven, Lord. Please help me go to heaven. I love you so much. Please let everything be okay. I will do what you say.'

I blink three times, visualise God in his big armchair, and kiss heaven, to make sure He's heard me. After the nightly ritual is finished, my eyes anxiously move from star to star, trying to really feel God and His home. I imagine my body rising closer to the dome of black and can feel the stars stretching out in a huge embrace around Robin Avenue and my family. There is robust, meticulous love. Storytime, Our Father, Hail Mary, Glory Be, Now I Lay Me, Prayers for Family, Goodnight Song, Drink of Water in the Yellow Cup, One Minute Snuggling Time, and 'Goodnight. I love you.' The love is unmistakable, kneaded into each child since we were born to the family, the loyalty there without deciding, method unquestioned: traditional, logical, right.

Suddenly, I feel myself parting from my parents and Iko downstairs, from Eduardo next door, being pulled toward sky and future and God more powerfully than ever before. I feel God telling me I am completely separate from everyone on Earth, and tied only to Him and His will. The tingle comes again, this time with excitement. Eyes closed in benediction, deep breaths and the vow 'I will do everything for you. I love you.'

After several minutes, I lie back down and can't stop smiling, the breeze and the dancing curtain so exciting to my South Texan skin.

THE COLOURING OF EGGS   LINDA MCKENNA

The little broken houses. Bluer
than the sky, the virgin's cloak,
newborn nurseries. So blue
they make a new name,
are carried away.
To confuse predators,
stop the tiny, ugly babies
from injuring themselves,
keep the place clean.
Or the mother bird eats them
to replenish calcium.
The blue was made last
in the long day it took
to build the egg and
comes from biliverdin,
which also makes bile;
the stuff of vomit and anger.

Take in the bitter with
the calcium, you will need it.
So many of these babies
will never make it;
will never put on weight
or feathers, will fall
into cats' mouths, will freeze.
Maybe better your plundered
ancestors lying in careful
nested drawers in guilty
unvisited corners.
I count 212 in the varnished
cabinets; keyless music boxes
whose song I can't shake off.

MAGNETISM   MEL WHITE

It's more than Leonard Cohen
rhyming do ya with hallelujah;

more than the way George Carlin
spoke about the stress of war,

then joked, in the next breath,
about toilet paper;

more than the Fibonacci sequence;
more than think global act local;

more than North and South poles –
drawn together, held apart;

more than prose;
more than the juxtaposition

of conflicting emotions in poems
that can't be paraphrased;

more than gravity; more than Eureka;
more than the combination

of wine press and coin punch
that inspired the printing press;

more than joining the dots
to map the constellations.

LOVING THE GLASS BLOWER   CHERYL PEARSON

I loiter in the hot shop, neglecting the boys with crushes
and trucks to watch him manipulate glass into shapes. The way
he bends the glass to his will, like water bending light to feed

the weed's hunger and stripe its fish. I've seen him suck
a cigarette, eyes closed like a sill-sunned cat's. I've seen him
bless the boy with a rose and pistol crossed on his chest

with the same mouth, the same kiss. My one flaw is the flaw
of my sex. I dream he melts me to caramel in his furnace,
uses his breath to amend my shape. Spark and char. The muscled

bunch of his arms, my arms. What light there is in the world. The light
carried in snow. The light a block of glass holds, or a glacier
shuttles from cap to cap on its blue route. Icarus fell, but he also

flew. The sun's tongue on his wax straps. The joy and terror of the heat.
I know it too. To love is to open like a flower. To love is to roll in salt
after peeling out of your skin. Each paperweight glows as he moulds it.

Each paperweight blooms with trammelled air. The one I steal
is the colour of fire. The seam of flame in a hot coal. Let me fall
with his breath in my curled fist. The hurt of it. The miracle.

SINGLE FILE — SIMON PERCHIK

Single file the way every stone
promises its last dance to the dead
who listen for beginners: small stones

a mourner leaves – in the dark
your grave more than the usual
smelling from an old love note

whose words you have forgotten
died all at the same time
as moonlight: a silence

you could hold in your hand
– you think it's the rain that stopped
though you are entitled to a tree

left here by its shade setting out
to fill itself with you, become a night
where there was none before.

THE CRANNÓG QUESTIONNAIRE   MIKE MCCORMACK

How would you introduce yourself as a writer to those who may not know you?

A writer of short stories and novels whose fundamental impulse is astonishment and who is always looking for new angles, structures and rhythms with which to make sense of this crazy world.

When did you start writing?

In my early twenties. I was studying Philosophy at the time in UCG as it was then but gradually my mind started turning towards writing fiction. I had my first piece of fiction published in the *Connacht Tribune* by Eva Bourke.

Do you have a writing routine?

Yes, loads of them but they never hold for more than a couple of days – something always happens to interrupt them. Life, in all its rowdy mood swings, keeps cutting across any routine I try to put in place. That said, I always find myself writing late at night ...

When you write, do you picture somehow a potential audience or do you just write?

I just write the book that comes to me. As a writer I have always felt that my first obligation is to the book I am writing. When the book is finished then I pray that it will find an audience.

Some writers describe themselves as planners, while others plunge right in to the writing. Would you consider yourself a planner or a plunger?

Plunge straight in, head first, and see what happens. For better or worse that's the way it has always been with me. I sometimes wonder had I been more of a planner would I have written more.

How important are names to you in your books? Do you choose the names based on liking the way they sound or for the meaning? Do you have any name-choosing

resources you recommend?

Names are very important – names of characters and names of stories are equally important to me. It is a strange thing, but I can recognise the proper name of a short story or novel the moment it presents itself. It kinda locks into position and steadies the whole thing and never moves thereafter. Characters' names are the same – I recognise them instantly, they fit properly and never move or wobble after that. The names of stories and characters always present themselves at that decisive moment in composition when my mind and imagination has clarified and come to terms with the piece.

Is there a certain type of scene that's harder for you to write than others? Love? Action? Erotic?

Love scenes are difficult. Everything delicate and fleet about love makes it hard to pin down in words. I have to approach love scenes very gingerly or else they tend to fly all over the place on me in big glutinous lumps.

Tell us a bit about your non-literary work experience, please?

For the past twenty years I have worked as a teacher of writing – undergrad, postgrad and on adult education courses. However, when writing my first book, which took up my whole twenties, I had such a varied selection of under-the-counter jobs – window cleaner, floorsweep, working on sites, dishwasher ... None of those jobs were very skilled but it was all good work which gave me the headspace in which to think about my first stories. I look back now and realise how valuable that headspace was.

What do you like to read in your free time?

I have a real fondness for short, snappy and well-plotted thrillers. I admire any writer who can construct a plot which is a credible, dramatic extension of the characters' lives.

What one book do you wish you had written?

Speaking as a writer from within the broad circumference of Ireland and Britain the novel of the last twenty years I admire most is *Destiny* by Tim Parks. This short novel really pushed my envy button when I read it. It still does to this day.

Do you see writing short stories as practice for writing novels?

No, it is a completely different discipline and it makes completely different demands of the writer. And what is good in the short story is more likely than not bad in the novel.

Do you think writers have a social role to play in society or is their role solely artistic?

My thinking on this swings back and forth. At the moment, I am convinced that writers have an obligation to be decent people, same as anyone else and that decency automatically puts them on the side of social issues like justice and equality. Whether or not that means that writers should be taking to the street leading great social movements I am not so sure – the twentieth century is full of writers who took up public positions on issues which, with the passage of time, now look lamentable.

Tell us something about your latest publication, please?

The last thing I 'published' was a short story broadcast by the BBC back in March. It was called *I, The Flock*, and it is one of a series of science fiction stories I am trying to write about an alternative Mayo – the world badly needs an alternative Mayo.

Can writing be taught?

No, thank God, and anyone who tells you otherwise is only codding you. That is the first thing I tell any of the classes I have to 'teach' – it can't be taught. I tell them to lay aside any notion of instruction or guidance and to put in place a working idea of experiment and exploration. Students respond much better to that idea and that is their first step towards finding their own voice.

Have you given or attended creative writing workshops and if you have, share your experiences a bit, please?

I've never been in a creative writing workshop – they were not really a thing in my generation. Maybe I would have gone if they had been available, but they weren't.

Flash fiction – how driven is the popularity of this form by social media like Twitter and its word limits? Do you see Twitter as somehow leading to shorter fiction?

I am not at all sure how much flash fiction is driven by social media. What does interest me is the correlation between this world of digital immediacy and the patience – readerly and writerly patience – needed to pursue the longer narrative art forms. Years of reading the manuscripts of younger writers convinces me that the generation behind me move at a much quicker beat and rhythm which seems to me to be taken from the instantaneous pulse of social media platforms. Sentences are shorter and snappier, scenes fly by in a blur. That is not a criticism of those rhythms, it is an observation that the world moves at a different pace for those young writers.

Finally, what question do you wish that someone would ask about your writing, and how would you answer it?

Hmmmm ... difficult one. How about 'Would you like a big huge advance for your next novel?' The answer to that is fairly obvious.

Finally, finally, some Quick Pick Questions:

E-books or print?

Print, for God's sake!

Dog or cat?

Dog. I am a fervent loather of cats.

Reviews – read or don't read?

Used to read but don't anymore.

Best city to inspire a writer: London Dublin New York (Other)?
Lisbon.

Favourite meal out: breakfast, lunch, dinner?
Breakfast, now that I think of it.

Weekly series or box sets?
Box sets I suppose.

Favourite colour?
All the blues.

Rolling Stones or Beatles?
Led Zeppelin

Night or day?
Half and half.

Artist's Statement

Cover image: *Tempus frangit tempus ducit* by Marie-Jeanne Jacob

Marie-Jeanne Jacob works a lot with comics and illustration. She studied Art in Ireland, New Zealand, Australia and Mexico, and Art and Education in Montreal, culminating in an illustrated thesis.

She has had installations in various festivals, co-ordinated children's festivals and camps, and exhibited in group and solo exhibitions. She has worked on murals abroad, and presented her work with comics and mental health at the Graphic Medicine Conference in Brighton and Sussex Medical School, Johns Hopkins medical campus, and the University of Dundee.

One of her main interests regarding practical studio work is the creation of spaces and the idea of the in-between, and she is fascinated by the use of comics within patient care, medical settings and education. She was the Artist-in-Residence at the Waterford Healing Arts Trust in 2015, and has run comics creation workshops in hospitals, care centres, mental health settings, and with Headway.

At the moment she is wrapping up a project involving 43 artists from all over the world, which she has been curating since 2015. She also really likes Roller Derby.

mariejjacob@gmail.com
http://mariejeannejacob.blogspot.ie
https://www.facebook.com/mariejeannejacob.art

Biographical Details

Kim Bridgford is the director of Poetry by the Sea and the editor of *Mezzo Cammin*. The author of nine books, she is the recipient of grants from the National Endowment for the Arts, the Connecticut Commission on the Arts, and the Ucross Foundation. Her three-volume series with visual artist Jo Yarrington, *The Falling Edge*, on their trips to Iceland, Venezuela, and Bhutan is forthcoming. She is known as 'America's First Lady of Form'.

Sandra Bunting lives in eastern Canada. Her latest book of short stories, *Everything in this House Breaks*, comes out this year.

Jane Burn's poems have been featured in magazines such as *The Rialto, Under The Radar, Butcher's Dog, Iota Poetry, Bare Fiction* as well as anthologies from the Emma Press, Beautiful Dragons, Fairacre Press, Emergency Poet and Seren.

David Butler is a multi-award-winning poet, playwright and novelist. His most recent novel, *City of Dis* (New Island), was shortlisted for the Kerry Group Novel of the Year 2015. His short stories have won the Maria Edgeworth twice, Fish International and ITT/Redline Awards.

Andrew Caldicott featured in the 2010 Poetry Ireland Introductions Series, and his work has appeared in numerous journals including *The Stony Thursday Book, The Stinging Fly, Southword, West47 Online, Crannóg, The Scaldy Detail, Shamrock Haiku Journal, Revival*, and *Boyne Berries*. Collaborative work has appeared in *Moonset* and the *Journal of Renga and Renku*.

Natalie Crick has poetry published in *Interpreters House, Poetry Scotland, THE SHOp, The High Window*, and *London Grip*. She is studying for an MA in Writing Poetry at Newcastle University, taught by Tara Bergin and Jacob Polley. Her poetry has been nominated for the Pushcart Prize twice.

Clive Donovan devotes himself full-time to poetry and has published in a wide variety of magazines including *Agenda, Interpreters House, The Transnational, Prole, Erbacce, Salzburg Review*, and in several online.

Saddiq Dzukogi holds a degree in Mass Communication from Ahmadu Bello University, Zaria. He is the author of *Inside the Flower Room*, selected by Kwame Dawes and Chris Abani for the APBF New Generation African Poets Chapbook Series. He was shortlisted for the 2017 Brunel International African Poetry Prize. His poems appear or are forthcoming in *Kenyon Review, New Orleans Review, South Dakota Review, Crab Orchard Review, Prairie Schooner, Best American Experimental Writing Series*, and *Verse Daily*. He is also a fellow of the Ebedi International Writers Residency.

Tanya Farrelly is the author of two books: *When Black Dogs Sing*, a short story collection (Winner of the Kate O'Brien Award 2017), and *The Girl Behind the Lens*, a literary thriller published by Harper Collins. Her stories have won prizes and been shortlisted in many competitions, among them the Hennessy Awards, the RTÉ Francis MacManus Awards, the Cúirt New Writing Prize and the William Trevor International Short Story Competition. Her stories have been widely published, appearing in literary journals such as the *Cúirt Annual*, the *Incubator Journal* and *Crannóg*. She has also read her work on RTÉ's *Sunday Miscellany* and *Arena*. In 2013 she completed a PhD in Creative and Critical Writing at Bangor University, Wales. She is the founder of STACCATO Spoken Word night, which she runs with her husband David Butler, and the organiser of Bray Literary Festival. A new novel is forthcoming in 2018.

Órla Fay is the editor of *Boyne Berries Magazine*. Recently her poetry has appeared in *Cyphers*, *Crossways Magazine*, *The Rose Magazine*, and *The Honest Ulsterman*. In 2017 she had poems shortlisted in The Dermot Healy International Poetry Competition and The Redline Book Festival Poetry Competition. She is currently undertaking the MA in Digital Arts and Humanities at UCC. She blogs at http://www.orlafay.blogspot.ie.

Mary Ellen Fean's poems have been published in *THE SHOp*, *Cyphers*, *The Galway Review*, *Revival*, *The Clare Champion* and broadcast on Clare FM radio. She was shortlisted for the Desmond O'Grady poetry prize in 2014. Her first collection, *Driftwood*, was published by Revival Press in 2018.

Olivia Fitzsimons was shortlisted for the Sunday Business Post/Penguin Short Story Prize, 2017, the Retreat West Flash Fiction Competition, 2017 and was longlisted for the Fish Short Story Prize, 2018.

Mary Melvin Geoghegan has four collections of poetry published. Her last is *Say it Like a Paragraph* (2012), Bradshaw Books, Cork. Her next collection, *As Moon and Mother Collide*, is due from Salmon Poetry. Her work has been published widely including *Poetry Ireland Review*, *Hodges Figgis 250th Anthology*, *Poem on the DART 2018*, *The Sunday Times*, *Crannóg*, *Skylight 47*, *THE SHOp*, *Cyphers*, *The Moth*, *The Stinging Fly*, *The Stony Thursday Book* amongst others. In 2013 she won the Longford Festival Award for Poetry and was shortlisted in 2017 for the Fish Poetry Award.

Sheila Gorman lives in Dublin and has had several stories and poems published.

Kevin Graham's poems have appeared in *The Irish Times*, *Crannóg*, and *The Stinging Fly*. Smithereens Press published a chapbook *Traces* in 2016. He is working on his first collection.

S.K. Grout's work appears in *Landfall*, *Aesthetica Magazine*, *The Interpreter's House*, *L'Éphémère Review* and elsewhere. She tweets at @indeskidge.

Hanahazukashi is an English teacher and a member of Galway Writers' Workshop. She is currently working on a bildungsroman about her youth in Texas, the midwest, Japan, and Ireland.

Edel Hanley is currently a student on the MA programme in Modernities at University College Cork. She has previously been published in *Quarryman* literary journal and *Motley* magazine.

Mark Hart's book, *Boy Singing to Cattle* (Pearl Editions, 2013), won the Pearl Poetry Prize, was a finalist for the Massachusetts Book Award, and was named a 'Must-Read Book' by the Massachusetts Center for the Book in 2014. His second book, *The Joy of Blasphemy*, was recently released by Leveler's Press.

Deirdre Hines is an award-winning poet and playwright. She has won The Stewart Parker Award for Best New Play with Howling Moon's *Silent Sons* in 1992. Her first collection of poetry *The Language of Coats* was published by New Island Books and includes the poems which won The Listowel Collection, 2011. She has been shortlisted for The Patrick Kavanagh Award in 2010. New poems have appeared in magazines in the UK, India, America and Ireland. She is on the organising committee of North West Words in Letterkenny.

Wendy Holborow, born in South Wales, lived in Greece for 14 years where she edited *Poetry Greece*. Her poetry has been published internationally and placed in competitions. She recently gained distinction for a Master's in Creative Writing at Swansea University. Collections include: *After the Silent Phone Call* (Poetry Salzburg, 2015), *Work's Forward Motion* (2016) and *An Italian Afternoon* (Indigo Dreams, 2017) which was a Poetry Book Society Pamphlet Choice, Winter 2017/18.

Pamela Johnson's poems appear in magazines such as *Magma, Fenland Reed, POEM* and anthologies published by Seren, Templar, and Cinnamon. She has published three novels, most recently *Taking In Water*, 2016, which was supported by an Arts Council Writers' Award. She teaches fiction on the MA in Creative & Life Writing, Goldsmiths, University of London.

Martin Keaveney has been widely published in Ireland, the UK and the US. Fiction, poetry and flash may be found at *Crannóg, The Crazy Oik*, and *Burning Word* among many others. His play *Coathanger* was selected for development at the Scripts Ireland festival in 2016. He has a BA and MA in English and is currently a PhD candidate at NUIG.

John D. Kelly's work has been placed and commended in various competitions and has appeared in many literary publications including *Poetry Ireland Review, Magma, The Honest Ulsterman, O'Bheal Five Words, The Galway Review, The Stony Thursday Book, Boyne Berries, Fish Anthology*, etc. His manuscript was highly commended in the Patrick Kavanagh Poetry Award 2016.

Sean Kelly has been published in *The Moth Magazine, The High Window* and *Skylight 47*. He has been shortlisted for the *Cork Literary Review* Poetry Manuscript competition and has read his work widely. He is CEO at the Everyman Theatre, Cork.

Olivia Kenny McCarthy has poems published in a variety of literary journals. She was third prize-winner in the Allingham Poetry Competition in 2017 and was shortlisted for the Listowel Writers' Week Poetry Collection Competition in 2017.

Vanessa Kirkpatrick's first collection, *To Catch the Light*, won the inaugural John Knight Memorial Poetry Manuscript Prize and was Commended for the Anne Elder Award (2013). Her second collection, *The Conversation of Trees*, was published in 2017 by Hope Street Press.

Craig Kurtz has written and recorded poetry since 1979. Current endeavours include *Antick Comedies*, a versification of Restoration plays illustrated by Anni Wilson (http://antickcomedies.blogspot.com/) and *Wortley Clutterbuck's Deplorable Poems*, an opera buffa in two acts (http://craigkurtz.blogspot.com/). Recent work appears in *Artemis Journal*, *Garfield Lake Review*, and *The Helix Magazine*.

Anthony Lawrence's most recent collection, *Headwaters* (Pitt Street Poetry), won the 2017 Prime Minister's Award for Poetry. He is a Senior Lecturer at Griffith University, Queensland, where he teaches creative writing.

Mercedes Lawry has published poetry in such journals as *Poetry*, *Nimrod*, *Prairie Schooner*, and *Harpur Palate*. She has been nominated for a Pushcart Prize on three occasions. She has published two chapbooks. Her manuscript, *Small Measures*, was selected for the Vachel Lindsay Poetry Prize from Twelve Winters Press and will be published in 2018. She was a finalist for the 2017 Airlie Press Prize and the 2017 Wheelbarrow Press Book Prize. She has also published short fiction and essays as well as stories and poems for children.

V.P. Loggins is the author of *The Green Cup*, winner of the 2016 Cider Press Review Editors' Prize, *The Fourth Paradise* (Main Street Rag, 2010), and *Heaven Changes* (Pudding House Chapbook Book Series, 2007), as well as two critical books on Shakespeare. In addition to *Crannóg*, his poems have appeared in *The Baltimore Review*, *The Healing Muse*, *Poet Lore*, *Poetry Ireland Review*, and *The Southern Review*, among other journals.

Eamonn Lynskey's work has appeared in many leading magazines and journals. His third collection, *It's Time*, was published by Salmon Poetry in 2017.

Linda McKenna has had poems published in *A New Ulster*, *Skylight 47*, *Panning for Poems*, *Lagan Online*, *The Blue Nib*, *Poetry NI's FourXFour*, *Dodging the Rain*, *Poetry in Motion Community Arts Anthology* and forthcoming in *The Bangor Literary Journal*. She won the Seamus Heaney Award For New Writing in 2018.

A. Mahlon Reece's poetry and artwork have appeared in *The Windward Review*, *Stylus*, and *The Voices and Faces Project*.

Tamzin Mitchell is a proofreader and editor currently based in London. She holds an MFA from the University of New Hampshire, and her work has appeared or is forthcoming in *Five on the Fifth, cahoodaloodaling,* and *Not One of Us,* among others.

Esther Murbach studied languages, history and philosophy in Basel and Berlin. She has worked as a journalist and translator writing mainly in German. Since 2008 she has been a freelance author, has published four novels, one short story collection (bilingual) and one poetry collection (trilingual) in Switzerland. Her first English novel, *The Turtle Woman,* appeared in 2012. A bilingual collection of non-fiction, fiction and poetry, *Swiss Going on Irish,* was published in spring 2017. In Ireland her work has appeared in *The Galway Review,* and *The Galway Advertiser.* www.esthermurbach.ch.

Deirdre Nally's short stories have been published in the *Sunday Tribune,* and shortlisted for both the Hennessy New Writer and Emerging Writer awards. She was also a published finalist in the Irish Times/Powers Irish Whiskey Short Story competition.

Cheryl Pearson's poems have appeared in publications including *The Guardian, Southword, The High Window, Under The Radar, Poetry NorthWest,* and *The Interpreter's House.* She has twice been nominated for a Pushcart Prize. She also writes short fiction, and was highly commended in the Costa Short Story Awards 2017. Her first full poetry collection, *Oysterlight,* is available now from Amazon/Pindrop Press.

Simon Perchik is an attorney whose poems have appeared in *Partisan Review, Forge, Poetry, Osiris, The New Yorker* and elsewhere. His most recent collection is *The Osiris Poems* published by box of chalk, 2017. For more information, including free e-books, his essay titled *Magic, Illusion and Other Realities* see www.simonperchik.com.

Caitlyn Rooke is a painter. Her visual work is represented by Kildare Gallery. She has exhibited in Dublin, London, New York and Pittsburgh.

Michael G. Smith is a chemist. His poetry has been published or is forthcoming in *Borderlands: Texas Poetry Review, The Broken Plate, Cider Press Review, Crannóg, Nimrod, The Santa Fe Literary Review, Sin Fronteras, Sulphur River Literary Review, Superstition Review,* and other journals and anthologies. *The Dark is Different in Reverse,* a chapbook, was published in 2013. *No Small Things,* a full-length book of poetry, was published by Tres Chicas Books in 2014. *The Dippers Do Their Part,* a collaboration with visual artist Laura Young of haibun and katagami, was published in 2015. *Flip Flop,* a volume of haiku co-authored with Miriam Sagan, was published in 2017. The Oregon Poetry Association selected his poem *Disturbance Theory* for the fall 2017 New Poets Award.

Adam Tavel won the 2017 Richard Wilbur Book Award for his third poetry collection, *Catafalque* (University of Evansville Press, 2018). He is also the author of *The Fawn Abyss* (Salmon Poetry, 2017) and *Plash & Levitation* (University of Alaska Press, 2015), winner of the Permafrost Book Prize in Poetry. http://adamtavel.com/.

Iain Twiddy grew up at the edge of the fens in Lincolnshire, eastern England. He lived for ten years in northern Japan, and has written two studies of contemporary poetry.

Andrea Ward's articles and book reviews have appeared in theological and education journals. She is a contributor to RTÉ's *Sunday Miscellany*. Her poetry has been published in *Crannóg* and is forthcoming in issue 10 of *Skylight 47*.

Jennifer Waring has an MA in Creative and Professional Writing from Roehampton University London, and is an international school IB English Language and Literature Teacher. Her poems have been shortlisted for *The Purple Breakfast Review* and commended in The Oriel Davies Open Writing Competition.

Mel White won the Éigse Michael Hartnett Poetry Slam in 2017 and was shortlisted for Listowel Writers' Week poetry competition. In 2016 she won the Cúirt Festival of Literature Poetry Slam and was placed second in the Tower Poetry Slam. Her poems have recently been published in *Dodging the Rain*, *Silver Streams Journal*, and *Stanzas*.

Emily Woodworth graduated in 2016 from Pacific University with a degree in Creative Writing. She has been published in *Literary Juice* and *Under the Sun*, and has a piece forthcoming in Broad Street. In addition, she writes screenplays and sketches with her brother, including their series *The Barista Times*.

Stay in touch with

Crannóg

@

www.crannogmagazine.com

Lightning Source UK Ltd.
Milton Keynes UK
UKHW01f1813100618
324021UK00002B/160/P